Lynching At Broken Butte

Lynching At Broken Butte

LEWIS B. PATTEN

DOUBLEDAY & COMPANY, INC.

GARDEN CITY, NEW YORK

1974

All of the characters in this book
are fictitious, and any resemblance
to actual persons, living or dead,
is purely coincidental.

Library of Congress Cataloging in Publication Data

Patten, Lewis B.
Lynching at Broken Butte.

I. Title.
PZ4.P316Ly [PS3566.A79]   813'.5'4
ISBN 0-385-05180-8
Library of Congress Catalog Card Number 73–22536

First Edition

Lynching At Broken Butte

CHAPTER 1

In the blistering heat of midday, the stage came down the long grade past the towering landmark known as Broken Butte and into the town of the same name at its foot, rocking on its thoroughbraces, jolting with the roughness of the road, and despite the lowered curtains, filling with a cloud of fine reddish dust as it slowed.

August Cragg sat limp in the forward-facing seat, having learned long ago that tenseness and bracing against the punishment inflicted by the stage only made it worse. He was bony and tall and, after five days on the stage in which the temperature at noon exceeded 120°, looked fifteen years older than the forty-five he admitted to. He wore wrinkled and soiled tan canvas pants, a faded blue woolen army shirt to which his United States Marshal's badge was pinned and a black-and-white striped vest that was frayed and gray with dust. The hat tipped forward over his gaunt, unshaven face was stained with sweat around the base of the crown and its brim was pulled down to a point in front.

The stage jolted to a halt in front of the stage depot on Main and the agent came out of the station and opened the door. Gus Cragg sat up straight, settled his hat on his head and waited while the agent helped the other passengers to alight. There was the round-faced Colt's Patent Arms Co. salesman with dust a mantle on his wrinkled blue serge suit who sat closest to the door and was the first one out. There was the hatchet-faced, middle-aged woman who had stared more or less disapprovingly at the other passengers throughout the trip and whose mouth was habitually compressed into a thin, straight line. And there was the little boy with her at whom Cragg had winked occasionally and who looked listless and miserable. The fourth passenger out was a hard-faced man of thirty who had avoided speaking to anyone and who had usually managed to avoid directly meeting Gus Cragg's glance.

Cragg uncoiled his six feet two and eased himself out of the coach. It was like coming out of an oven into a furnace. He winced and stepped out of the sun immediately, thinking that forty-five was getting pretty old for this kind of life and that he ought to quit. The hell of it was, he didn't have enough saved to live and he didn't know what else he could do. He'd been a lawman since he'd turned eighteen, starting as a town marshal's deputy in Kansas and working up gradually to the job he held now.

He waited beneath the shade of the gallery overhang until all the other passengers had gone inside and then he followed them.

The interior, by comparison with the outdoors, was cool. And dark. There was a bare wooden floor, its varnish worn off where the wear was heaviest. Coarse Mexican rugs were scattered here and there. The furniture was heavy and leather-covered and in one corner there was a long table with chairs on either side and at both ends. A stairway led to the second floor, where there were rooms for passengers who stayed overnight.

Two women were busy setting the table. The station agent said in a loud, nasal voice, "Washbasins and outhouses out in back, folks. Dinner will be on in ten minutes or so."

Cragg walked past the man as he headed out to wash. The agent saw the badge on his vest and for a moment there was pure panic in his eyes. Cragg thought he was going to bolt, but he didn't. He swallowed and turned away and Cragg, after searching his memory for some recognition of the man, went on his way. He'd encountered the same reaction before and knew that usually it meant the man had something criminal in his past.

But a lot of men had such things in their pasts and past misdeeds were no concern of Cragg's. He worked what he was assigned to work and let the rest alone unless he happened to interrupt the commission of a crime, or unless he was looking for a particular man.

The yard behind the stage depot was as hot as it had been in the street. Cragg went to the outhouse, waited his turn, then returned and pumped a basin half full of lukewarm water from the well. He washed, dried on the dirty towel, ran his fingers through his graying hair and went back inside.

The station agent had disappeared. Cragg followed the woman and boy to the table and took a seat across from them. He picked up each serving dish after the woman had finished serving the boy and herself, helped himself, then passed it on to the Colt's salesman next to him.

He thought of the heat outside, wincing inwardly at the prospect of going into it again. He considered the physical beating he knew he would take this afternoon from the lurching, jolting coach and he thought how nice it would be to spend the afternoon here, or in the town saloon drinking beer, or sleeping upstairs in one of the rooms.

Wryly he thought that as little as five years ago, such concerns wouldn't have troubled him. He'd have gone on, with little thought of the discomfort, enduring it without undue suffering.

But this wasn't five years ago and there was no real reason why he had to punish himself. A stage went through

Broken Butte every other day. He could lay over and go out day after tomorrow and nobody the worse for it. His assignment was to proceed to Fort Apache, Arizona, pick up a prisoner and return him to Fort Worth. The prisoner was safe in the post stockade and would keep until he could arrive.

Having decided to remain in Broken Butte until the next westbound stage came through, he relaxed and let himself enjoy the dinner, hot as it was. Once, as he ate, he remembered the look of panic that had been in the station agent's eyes but because it was of no consequence to him, he put it out of his mind.

Clifton Kubec, the station agent, was a man of medium size, five feet eight inches tall. He had worked for the Butterfield Stageline going on seven years. He made what he considered to be a good salary and he had a comfortable amount in the Broken Butte bank. He was a bachelor, a substantial citizen.

But the sight of the U. S. Marshal's badge had put a cold chill of fear into him. As soon as the gaunt, big man disappeared through the rear door, he went out the front into the blistering heat of the street.

Broken Butte, despite the fact that it was the county seat, was not very large. Main Street was two blocks long, lined with business establishments on both sides, terminating at Dry Creek which it crossed on a wooden bridge and beyond became a dusty road leading east past towering Broken Butte.

There were residential streets on both sides of Main, and these streets were designated First, Second, Third, and Fourth. The cross streets were Cottonwood, down by the bridge, Willow, farther up, and Maple. The last cross street at the west end of town was no more than a dusty alley and had no name.

A total of eighty-one people lived in Broken Butte, and the town survived by serving the ranches that surrounded it. Weekdays, the town was quiet, almost sleepy, but on Saturday it came alive when riders and buckboards filled its streets. Saturday night never ended until 2 A.M. on Sunday when Sheriff Jasper Horsley closed the saloon.

The courthouse was a two-story frame building facing Main between Cottonwood and Willow. Snuggled against its side was the sheriff's office and jail, built of red sandstone with iron-barred windows and a sod roof laid over poles and brush. The courthouse had been built a dozen years after the jail.

Kubec hurried to the door of the jail and burst inside. His face was shiny with sweat and red from the heat. He said excitedly, "There's a U. S. Marshal in town! Came in on the stage!"

Horsley glanced up from his desk. He was a broad and powerful man who looked older than his forty years because his head was bald. He had a wide mustache that drooped at the corners of his mouth and hid most of it. He scowled. "So what? He's likely just passing through."

"Maybe he ain't. Maybe . . ."

Horsley said, "Shut up. Go on back. No use getting all heated up before we know. I'll come and take a look at him if he's still here after the stage pulls out."

Kubec's mouth worked as if he would say something else but no words came out. At last he turned and went back outside. He hurried toward the stage station farther up the street.

Horsley got up and went to the window. He watched Kubec go up the street and saw him disappear into the stage depot. There was a faintly worried frown on the sheriff's face. He didn't know how the marshal could have found out but it was possible that he had. Eighty-one people lived here. Not all of them had been involved. One might have written a letter. But there was no use worrying, at least until the stage pulled out at one. If the marshal was on it, fine. If he wasn't, there was time enough to worry then.

Despite his own self-reassurances he began to pace back and forth and he began to sweat. Even with the stone walls and sod roof, it was 90° inside the jail. He stopped and forced himself to sit down at his desk. He packed and lighted his pipe and filled the room with a blue haze of smoke. He looked at the clock on the wall. It was only a quarter after twelve.

He still didn't blame himself for what had happened five months ago. He simply made a choice between his friends and neighbors, the people who had elected him, and two strangers who didn't mean a thing to him. It was a choice any reasonable man would have made.

At least that was what he told himself. But when he was alone he often asked himself why, if that was so, had nightmares tormented his sleep every night for the last five months? Why didn't he have friends in Broken Butte any more? Why was he writing letters, looking for another job?

Because he knew he couldn't stay. Because he'd never be elected here again. Because he could never forget what he must forget if he was to remain.

He got up and began to pace again. He looked at the clock. It must have stopped, he thought when he saw the hands. More than five minutes had to have elapsed since Kubec left. But the clock hadn't stopped.

What would he do if the marshal stayed? He'd have to assume the marshal had been summoned here. And then he'd have to make another choice.

•

From the window he watched the sweated teams that had drawn the coach into Broken Butte replaced with fresh teams from the livery barn at the foot of Main. He watched the driver uncover the luggage boot and take out a single grip. He put it on the boardwalk under the gallery.

The sheriff's mind went back to that black night five months ago and the tempo of his pacing involuntarily increased. Back and forth he went. Back and forth.

What could he do, he asked himself, if the U. S. Marshal stayed? Well, for starters, he'd go up and introduce himself. He could try and draw the man out and find out how much he knew.

His sweat felt clammy and cold in spite of the heat inside the room. He watched the clock, watched the hands inexorably move toward one o'clock.

At last he saw the passengers straggle listlessly from the stage depot. A woman and boy came first, followed by a medium-sized man in ranch clothes. The fourth passenger to board looked like some kind of salesman.

The driver climbed up to the seat. He cracked his long whip over the teams and the coach began to move, leaving a cloud of dust hanging in the street.

The man in range clothes could have been the marshal, Horsley supposed. But he didn't think so.

Someone had stayed behind. He saw Kubec come from the stage depot, saw him pick up the grip the driver had placed on the boardwalk and saw him carry it inside. Kubec threw a glance toward the jail as he did.

Horsley didn't want to do it but he knew it must be done. He had to know if the marshal had stayed in town. He had to introduce himself and offer his help if the marshal needed it.

He pulled a bandanna from his pocket and mopped his face. He took his hat off the coat tree by the door and settled it on his head. He stepped out into the furnace heat of the street, wincing when the sun struck him like a blow.

He walked slowly and reluctantly uptown toward the stage depot. The stage had disappeared but its dust cloud lingered over the main street of Broken Butte and over the road beyond.

Horsley stopped beneath the gallery in front of the stage depot. His mouth felt dry and he looked longingly toward the saloon across the street. Licking his lips he went inside.

He saw the marshal, still sitting at the dinner table. He had finished eating and was idly picking his teeth. Horsley shoved his hat back on his head, squared his shoulders and approached the man.

He knew his hand would be clammy when he shook the marshal's hand, but he hoped he could meet and hold the man's glance. He hoped his voice would come out normally.

CHAPTER 2

The marshal looked up as Horsley approached. Horsley said quickly, "Don't get up. It's too damned hot." He put out his hand and the marshal took it and Horsley knew it was sweaty and clammy and pulled it back as soon as he could. The marshal was looking questioningly at him and Horsley said, "I heard you were in town. Came up to pay my respects and see if there was anything I could do."

The marshal's eyes were grayish and calm and seemed to probe into Horsley's thoughts. The marshal said, "Nope. I guess there's nothing you can do."

"You staying long?"

The marshal shrugged. He calmly studied Horsley and the sheriff tried desperately to hold his glance. He failed and looked away, then busied himself with packing and lighting his pipe to hide the fact that he had. He knew his fingers were shaking but he'd started and had to finish or reveal his nervousness.

Suddenly all he wanted was to get away. He knew why the marshal had come to Broken Butte. Someone had written a letter and the whole thing was going to come out.

He got to his feet. "Well, if there's anything . . ." and let the sentence trail away, unfinished.

The marshal said, "I'll let you know."

Horsley escaped as quickly as he could. Sweating copiously, he hurried back down the street to the jail.

He thought about leaving town, then discarded the idea.

He hadn't done anything so bad. He'd only made a choice. between the people of this community and a couple of prisoners he'd honestly thought to be guilty of the crime of which they were accused. Maybe he hadn't made the right decision, but at least what he'd done wasn't criminal. He couldn't be charged and tried.

The marshal was after the ones who could be charged and tried and that was close to half the men in town. Horsley began to pace back and forth, sweating and puffing furiously on his pipe.

Puzzled, Gus Cragg watched Horsley hurry to the door. He didn't know what was going on. He couldn't understand why everyone was so scared. Their fear interested him, but only because of curiosity. He didn't intend to probe. His job was to pick up a prisoner at Fort Apache and return him to Fort Worth. He intended to do that and only that.

He thought of climbing the stairs and sleeping through the afternoon but he knew how hot the upstairs rooms would be. He'd never sleep in that heat unless he first had a couple of drinks.

He got up. He left a quarter on the table to pay for his meal. He wandered through the lobby to the door. He felt like he was being watched, but when he turned his head, nobody was watching him.

He stepped out into the blistering heat of the street. It was deserted. Not even a dog stirred along its dusty length. Cragg looked down the street toward the saloon. The swinging doors were in shadow, shielded from the sun by a covered gallery.

He crossed the street. The heat, reflected up from the dry, deep dust, was nearly intolerable, but he didn't hurry. He reached the boardwalk on the far side, stepped up to it. His footsteps echoed briefly against its hollowness. Then he crossed Willow and stepped inside the saloon.

Instantly he knew they also had been watching him. The place was as silent as a tomb. There were five men inside the place, besides the bartender. He glanced at each as he walked the half-dozen steps to the bar.

The bartender approached him warily. Cragg asked, "You got any beer?"

The bartender nodded.

"How cold is it?"

The bartender shrugged, then said, "Colder than out there."

Cragg nodded. The bartender brought out a brown bottle and opened it. He slid it to Cragg, along with a glass. The neck of the bottle foamed over onto the bar. Cragg poured the glass half full.

He could feel the men in the saloon watching him, but whenever he turned his head, they quickly looked away. A faint irritation came to him and he wondered why everyone was so damned afraid. He wished he'd continued on the stage. Even the heat would have been better than being watched like this. He quickly gulped the beer, ordered another and gulped that too. He left a dime on the bar and turned toward the door.

The bartender's voice stopped him. "That's a U. S. Marshal's badge, ain't it?"

He turned his head. "Yes. Why?"

"Just curious."

Cragg waited a moment to see if anyone else would speak. He started toward the door again, only to be stopped a second time. "How long you stayin' in Broken Butte?"

He didn't answer that. He went on toward the doors, through them and out into the sun.

The beer had been strong and the heat magnified its effect. He was a little lightheaded but he knew part of it could be weariness. He felt sleepy now and crossed the street to the stage depot.

The station agent moved back away from the door as he came in, pretending to be disinterested. Cragg said, "I want a room."

"Yes, sir."

"You got one in front?"

"Yes, sir." The agent crossed the room and took a key from a rack of cubbyholes. He gave it to Cragg without meeting his glance.

Cragg picked up his grip and went up the stairs. There were numbers on the rooms. His was the third on the street side of the hall. He unlocked the door and went inside.

He closed the door and locked it, then pocketed the key. He put down his grip and walked to the window. The room was stifling and half a dozen blue-bodied flies buzzed against the dirty glass. He opened the window and stared down into the street. It was as deserted as before but he had the sure feeling that he was being watched by unseen eyes.

He unbuckled his gunbelt and laid it on the floor beside the bed. He pulled off his boots and laid down on his back. He stared at the cracked and peeling ceiling for a moment before he closed his eyes.

Something had happened here and he knew he ought to look into it. His head whirled. The flies buzzed against the window. One circled the room, droning as it did.

Gus Cragg sweated helplessly. But, as his clothes became drenched with sweat, the evaporative action cooled him enough for him to get to sleep. He began to snore.

The blistering sun traveled across the western sky and

with maddening slowness settled toward the horizon in the west. Gus Cragg slept on.

Eric Carberry was a tall, powerfully built man in his early fifties. He had a genial look about his homely face, but if a person watched him for any length of time, it became readily apparent that his surface geniality was only that. Carberry came across after some study as a nervously dynamic man with a powerful personality and all the geniality of a rattlesnake.

He owned the mercantile store, the livery stable, and the bank, which he operated from the back room of the store. An ambitious man, he enjoyed his position in the community and the county at least as much as he enjoyed his wealth, which was more considerable than even the townspeople who knew him best supposed.

Jasper Horsley brought him the news that the marshal was in town. Pipe held tightly in his teeth, Horsley came into the store in early afternoon and went straight to Carberry's office in the back room of the store. He said, "There's a U. S. Marshal in town. Came in on the stage and stayed."

"Why? What does he want?"

Horsley stared at him. Until five months ago he'd always acted with deference toward Carberry because he knew remaining as sheriff required it. Carberry could make or break a man. Nobody but a fool would forget that obvious fact of life. Lately it didn't seem to matter any more. Besides the marshal was going to bust this thing wide open. Even Carberry's money and position couldn't help. He said, "I didn't ask, but I figure it's plain enough. He knows what happened here five months ago. He's come to dig out the truth."

"We can't be sure of that." Carberry's eyes were sharp and hard, his mouth compressed.

"Why else would he get off the stage and stay?"

Carberry shrugged. "Might be any of a dozen reasons."

"I can't think of any."

Carberry fixed him with his stare. His eyes were like two marbles and his face was cold. "Don't lose your nerve."

Carberry could say so damned many things without actually putting them into words, thought Horsley. He could threaten you, or show contempt, or worse, make you feel like nothing at all. That was the way Carberry was making him feel right now. Defiance rose in Horsley. He said, "I didn't do anything. Don't you look at me like that."

Carberry said icily, "No. You didn't do anything. That's exactly the point. If you had, the people of this town wouldn't have done what they did."

Horsley said, "Oh no, by God! Don't you lay it all on me!"

"Who should I lay it on? If you'd done your job, those two would still be alive."

"And you and maybe half a dozen others who live in this town would be dead."

"We don't know that. Maybe a firm stand on your part would have turned us back."

Horsley looked him straight in the eye. He said distinctly, "You son-of-a-bitch!"

For an instant something flared in Carberry's eyes. Then it died. "Name calling isn't going to help."

"What *is* going to help?"

"If nobody talks, how is he going to find out anything?"

"You think nobody's going to talk? Hell, Kubec's about to come apart."

"Talk to him. Talk to the others too."

"Somebody will talk. Likely somebody already has. That's the only way he could have known."

"Maybe we'll have to get rid of him."

Horsley said harshly, "Kill him, you mean?"

"I didn't say that."

"But you meant it. Didn't you?"

Carberry shrugged. "It's one way out."

"You can't just up and kill a U. S. Marshal. He'd be missed. The stage driver would say he got off here."

"Not if he's persuaded not to talk."

Horsley looked at him in unbelief. "You mean kill him too?"

"Kill is your word, not mine."

"It still wouldn't do any good. He was sent here, remember?"

"Then we'll find another way."

"You find it. I'm out of it."

Carberry nodded. "You sure as hell are. You'll never be elected to another term."

Horsley said, "There are other jobs."

"Not for a man who's done what you did. Not lawman jobs anyway."

"Other jobs, then." He realized that he wanted to talk himself back into Carberry's good graces and he hated himself for it. He said, "Maybe I'll just talk to the marshal and tell him the whole dirty story."

Carberry's eyes were like bits of slate. "Don't."

That one simple word and Carberry's tone had the power to put a piece of ice in the sheriff's chest. He grumbled, "Hell, you know me better than that."

"I surely hope I do."

Horsley didn't meet his eyes again. He said surlily, "Well, I told you. Now it's up to you."

Carberry didn't reply and Horsley didn't wait. He went out of Carberry's office and walked along the aisle to the door. He stepped out into the heat, wondering why he still felt so cold.

He'd be glad to get away from here, he thought. He'd

be glad to take a different kind of job, where maybe he could eventually forget.

But he was sorry he'd called Carberry what he had. He was even more sorry he'd threatened to go to the marshal and tell him the whole story.

The strange chill stayed with him all the way to the jail and for a long time afterward. The fear that came with the chill stayed even after that.

CHAPTER 3

Eric Carberry stared angrily after the retreating figure of
the sheriff. He rarely frowned because it didn't fit his
image of geniality, but he was frowning now. If the U. S.
Marshal *was* here to investigate the two deaths five months
ago, then he was in trouble because it was he who had
incited the mob to what they did. Without him, they'd never
have gone through with it.

But damn it, his own daughter was the one who had been
killed. He swung his swivel chair around and stared at her
photograph sitting on his desk. Looking at her was painful
because it started him to remembering. It would have been
easier to put her photograph away, but then Carberry had
never sought the easy way.

The photograph showed a sweet-faced girl in braids with
a silk hair bow on the back of her head. She was sitting
demurely in a chair, hands folded in her lap.

Looking at her picture, Carberry remembered the fury
that had gone through him the night they carried her
body in off the prairie where they'd found her, wrapped in
nothing but the saddle blanket belonging to one of the
cowboys who discovered her. God, he'd wanted to get his
hands on the men who had killed her! He'd wanted that
more than he had ever wanted anything.

His eyes took on a strange, almost hypnotized look and
for this moment he was once again living that night five
months before . . .

He was just locking up when the two cowboys rode into town. They drew their horses to a halt in front of the courthouse down the street. One was carrying something across his saddle. Out of curiosity, Carberry walked that way.

There was a lamp burning in the sheriff's office. A square of light showed when the door was opened and the sheriff came hurrying out. He took the burden from the mounted man and carried it inside. The two riders followed him in. The sheriff closed the door.

Very curious now, Carberry tried the door of the jail and found it locked. He knocked and Sheriff Horsley came to the door. Carberry asked, "What's happening? Was that a body you just carried in?"

Horsley came out, closing the door behind him. He said, "Mr. Carberry, will you go get Doc Hebert for me? Tell him to bring some blankets besides what else he needs."

"Why? Is that a body you've got in there?"

"Yes sir, Mr. Carberry. I'm afraid it is."

"Who? It looked like the body of a child."

The sheriff seemed to poise himself as if to run. "I can't tell you . . ." He stopped, then blurted, "Jesus, Mr. Carberry, it's your girl Eloise!"

He said some more words, and he tried to restrain Eric Carberry, but he might just as well have tried to restrain a holocaust. Carberry burst into the office. The two cowboys stood in the corner of the room, talking in lowered tones and looking scared. Carberry stumbled to his daughter's body, lying on the sheriff's leather-covered couch. He flung himself down beside her and took her face between his hands, gently because it was bruised and lacerated. Both her eyes were swelled nearly shut.

He felt tears scalding his eyes and running across his cheeks to drop unheeded to the floor. Her face was cold, so there could be no doubt that she was dead.

How long he sat there, how long he sobbed out his grief, he could not have said. He had the remembrance of hushed voices in the room and later learned that the sheriff had been questioning the two who had discovered Eloise.

At last he released his daughter's face and got unsteadily to his feet. He wiped the tears from his cheeks and faced the sheriff. He asked harshly, "Who?"

"I don't know yet, Mr. Carberry. But I'll find out, you can count on that."

"When will you find out?"

"Can't read tracks in the dark but I know right where she was found. I'll be out there with a posse just as soon as it's light enough to trail."

"That ain't soon enough. What about the two that brought her in?"

"They're all right, Mr. Carberry. They work out at Turkey Track. Besides, if they'd had anything to do with it, they wouldn't have brought her in."

"Where are they now?"

"I sent 'em up to get Doc Hebert."

Carberry asked, "Who in God's name would do a thing like this?"

Horsley shook his head. "A crazy man, Mr. Carberry. It'd have to be a crazy man."

Carberry said, "I want him. By God, I want that son-of-a-bitch!"

"You'll get him, Mr. Carberry. I swear you will! I'll stay after him until I do get him."

"I'm going with you."

"All right, Mr. Carberry." The sheriff hesitated. "Hadn't you ought to go tell your wife?"

Carberry nodded dazedly. "Yes. I suppose I should."

Shock had numbed him and he found it difficult to think. Otherwise, he would have remembered the two saddle tramps that had been in town briefly this morning, who had left in midafternoon. He walked up the darkened street in a daze, only nodding absently as Doc Hebert passed him, hurrying, carrying a blanket and his bag.

The two cowboys were over at Sam Flagler's little house next door to the saloon, knocking on his door. When he opened it, they told him what had happened and asked him, for God's sake, to either open up or give them a bottle to get rid of the shakes. Finding a girl killed the way Eloise had been was more than either of them could stand.

Flagler's protests died when he heard what had happened. He came into the street in his nightshirt, carrying pants and boots, and opened up the saloon. A moment later a lamp glowed inside.

Carberry went on up the street to the big two-story white frame house at its upper end. The house sat back from the street, surrounded by browning lawn and a white picket fence. There was a lamp burning in the parlor window. The door was unlocked and he went inside.

His wife sat in her platform rocker, her sewing in her lap. She was a tiny, timid woman, awed by the size and power of her husband. She said, "I waited up for you, dear. Would you like something to eat?"

She saw his face, then, and came out of the chair, her sewing tumbling to the floor. "What's the matter?"

"It's Eloise. She's dead."

"How could that be? She's over at Nan Easterday's."

He shook his head. "She's dead."

She rushed at him like a bird attacking an animal threatening its nest. She beat at his face with her small clenched fists until he caught her wrists. "You're just trying to hurt me! You're doing this just because . . . !"

He released her wrists and seized her shoulders. He

shook her until her teeth rattled. He bawled, "Stop it! Damn you, stop it! I'm telling you the truth! Eloise is dead!"

Dead at fifteen. Dead in a way that had not been easy, that had taken a long, long time. But how had they gotten her? She had been at Nan Easterday's.

He swung around, leaving his wife standing there shocked, not yet in tears and hurried out the door. Down the dark street he went to the neat log cabin occupied by Clara Easterday and her daughter Nan, who was the same age Eloise had been.

He beat on the door until he heard frightened, protesting voices inside, then roared, "It's Eric Carberry! Open up!"

Clara Easterday opened the door, clad in a wrapper, a flowered cap over her head. Even just awakened, even in a shapeless wrapper and with a cap over her hair, she was a striking woman. Nothing could ever hide that fact. She was a widow and lived with her daughter. She operated the restaurant a few doors down the street from the stage depot. Carberry said hoarsely, "I thought Eloise was spending the night with Nan."

Clara Easterday looked confused. She saw the anger in Carberry, thought it was directed at her, and spoke with a bit of sharpness of her own. "This is the first I've heard of it."

"You haven't seen her at all tonight?"

"No. Why? Is something wrong?"

"She's dead," he said brutally. The truth was beginning to come to him. Eloise had lied about spending the night with Nan. At fifteen, she had been seeing some man secretly . . . At fifteen. He felt suddenly angry at her, for all that she was dead, because she had deceived him and lied to him.

Who had the man been, he wondered. Or had there been more than one? His fury grew as he rushed along the street, heading toward the jail again. Like a holocaust it grew. He'd never understood his daughter, nor his wife. He didn't understand them now. Eloise had been as rebellious as her mother was docile and obedient. She had always seemed to delight in doing the exact opposite of what she had been told to do. As if deliberately, to anger him.

But that didn't matter now. What mattered was finding the one who had murdered her.

The saloon doors were open and there were half a dozen lamps inside. He needed a drink himself and banged into the place. The two cowboys were standing at the bar, along with the sheriff and Doc Hebert. He looked at them both accusingly. "You left her alone down there?"

The sheriff shook his head. "We carried her over to Mrs. Littlejohn's. She said she'd dress her and take care of her."

Carberry looked at Flagler. "Give me a drink."

Flagler slid him a bottle and a glass. Carberry dumped whiskey into the glass with hands that shook so violently some of it spilled on the bar. He gulped the drink and poured another one. Eloise's death was a pain that would not go away, but even worse was the knowledge that she had deceived and lied to him, that she had been out on the prairie with some man, rolling in the dirt . . . His fist tightened on the glass with such force that it broke. He looked down dazedly at his cut and bleeding hand.

Doc opened his bag and took Carberry's hand. Flagler began to clean up the broken glass. All of them looked at him with a mixture of compassion and uncertainty.

Doc cleaned the cuts and wound bandages around the hand. Flagler put another glass out and filled it. Carberry picked it up with his left hand and drank it down. Doc Hebert said, "You ought to go home and try to sleep. I'll give you something . . ."

Carberry shook his head impatiently. "To hell with that!" He looked at Sheriff Horsley. "She was seeing someone. Do you know who it was?"

Horsley said, "She was a pretty girl. Half the boys in town . . ."

"I ain't talking about boys."

Horsley said, "I don't know of nobody."

"You're lying."

"No, sir. Why would I lie? I want the man that killed her too."

"Then get after him."

"Mr. Carberry, I can't do nothing until it gets light. If I take a posse out there now, they'll mess up all the tracks and might keep us from finding the man at all."

Carberry fumed helplessly. Suddenly he remembered the pair that had been in his store today. He said, "Those two saddle tramps! By God, they're the ones! They got to be!"

He didn't wait for the sheriff, Doc Flagler, and the two cowboys to either agree with him or disagree. He rushed out, crossed to the courthouse and ran inside. The door was unlocked, as were almost all the doors in Broken Butte. He ran up the stairs and into the little cubicle where the firebell was. He rang it frantically, stopping only when lamps began flickering in windows throughout the town, when people in various stages of dress ran into the streets. Then he left and descended the stairs again.

Horsley was waiting for him in front of the courthouse. "What are you doing? What's the use of waking everybody up?"

"We're going after those saddle tramps."

"How are you going to get them in the dark?"

"They said they were going north."

"If they killed your daughter, they'd go any way but north."

"How would they know she'd be found right away? They probably figured it would be days before anybody found her body and brought her in."

Horsley said, "Mr. Carberry, I'll get the man, whoever he is. But wait until it gets light."

Carberry's face was set in a harsh and angry mold. He turned to face the crowd that was gathering. The torment inside him was such that he had to relieve it and very soon. He bawled, "My little girl's been killed. We know who did it—those two saddle tramps that were in town today. I want some men to go with me."

He heard the murmuring that grew and grew until it filled the street. The crowd dispersed, the men hurrying home to get dressed, to saddle horses, to get weapons and provisions. Carberry bawled at their retreating backs, "Be back here in half an hour!"

Horsley said resignedly, "All right. We'll go after them. But we're bringing them back to jail. They're going to have a trial. Is that understood?"

Carberry didn't even bother to answer him.

CHAPTER 4

They left town at one in the morning, eleven strong. Carberry and Sheriff Horsley were in the lead, with the others staying close behind. They rode out on the rutted, two-track road whose only travel was by ranchers and their cowhands living north of town. The road wound across the rough and barren landscape for nearly forty miles before it petered out. Beyond was open desert for another twenty miles before another east-west road was reached.

Half a mile from town, Carberry hauled his horse to a plunging halt. The others nearly overran him, but stopped when he dismounted. He knelt in the middle of the dusty road and lit a match. Horsley got down with him and the two examined the surface of the road by the flaring light of matches. When they remounted, Carberry said, "It's them, the dirty sonsabitches! They likely didn't figure she'd be found for days."

Horsley said, "Maybe it wasn't them that killed her."

"Who the hell else could it have been? There ain't no other strangers within fifty miles of here."

"We don't know that."

"I know it."

"Then maybe it was somebody that lives in town."

Carberry said, "No!"

Horsley asked, "How come you didn't miss her, Mr. Carberry? I been wondering about that."

Carberry replied before he thought, "She was supposed to be staying with Nan Easterday."

"Supposed to be?"

Carberry said angrily, "What the hell's the matter with you? Why all the questions?"

Horsley said, "That's my job, Mr. Carberry. Asking questions. I'm supposed to find out what happened and who did it and I can't do that unless I know the facts."

"You know all the facts you need to know. You just put your mind on catching these two lousy killers."

Horsley was silent. Carberry was upset and angry and there was little sense in arguing with him now. But Horsley was wondering. Eloise Carberry hadn't been at home, and she hadn't been at Easterday's. She'd been somewhere in town or nearby and she hadn't been alone. Since she hadn't been taken from her home or from Easterday's by force, she must have gone wherever she had gone of her own free will. Supporting that theory was the fact that she had lied to her parents about where she was going to spend the night.

She therefore must have meant to spend the entire night with somebody and that person could have been the one who killed her.

He admitted that Eloise's unknown companion or companions could easily have been the two strangers they were following. Then, shaking his head, he tried to put the matter of Eloise's deception out of his mind. All he needed to do now was catch the strangers, bring them back to Broken Butte and lock them up in jail. It would be up to a judge and jury to decide whether or not they were guilty of killing Eloise.

About five miles from town, the road topped a shallow ridge and descended into a wide valley in the bottom of which was a wide, dry wash. Most times by digging down a couple of feet into the sand of the wash, water could be found, and apparently this was the reason for the two strangers camping here. On the near bank of the wash, the embers of a fire glowed, and as they swept down the slope, a horse nickered nervously below.

Carberry exulted, "We've got them, by God! We got the murdering bastards!"

Horsley didn't say anything. There wasn't any use. But he had the uneasy feeling that getting the strangers safely back to town might be a bigger job than he'd bargained for.

The galloping horsemen thundered into the strangers' camp, raising a blinding cloud of dust. The strangers were standing up, in underwear, surrounded and scared, apparently not understanding what was happening. Horsley spoke before anybody else could. "You two are under arrest. Get your clothes on and come on back to town."

One of the men said plaintively, "What for, for Christ's sake? We ain't done nothing."

Horsley said, "Get dressed and saddle up. Don't give me no arguments."

Carberry broke in. "Wait. Throw some wood on what's left of that fire. Let's get a look at these woman-killing bastards."

There was a pile of firewood beside the fire's embers. One of the men dismounted and fed the fire. The flames leaped up almost immediately. Both strangers were now desperately scared. One said, "You got somethin' wrong, mister. We ain't who you're looking for. We wouldn't kill nobody, let alone a woman. Honest to God, we ain't done nothing wrong."

Carberry swung ponderously from his horse. He approached the speaker. Without warning, he hit him squarely in the mouth with his fist. The man fell back, sprawling on the ground. Carberry was on him like a wolf.

Horsley roared, "Some of you pull him off! Goddammit, I'm not going to put up with this kind of thing! These men are my prisoners!"

It took four men to pull Carberry off. When they released him Carberry swung to face Horsley, white and furious. "The son-of-a-bitch has got scratches all over his face!"

Horsley dismounted. He walked to the stranger, gave him a hand and pulled him to his feet. There *were* scratches on the man's face, long, parallel scratches that had to have been made either by claws or fingernails. Horsley said, "Where'd you get scratched?"

The man was panicky. He swallowed twice before he could speak. "Saloon woman a day south of here. Came time to pay, I didn't have enough."

Horsley looked at Carberry. "They were in your store yesterday, Mr. Carberry. Did he have the scratches then?"

"No by God. I don't remember no scratches and I'd sure as hell have seen them if they'd been there!"

Horsley looked at the man. "What about it?"

"I never came face to face with him. He couldn't have seen whether I was scratched or not. Please, Sheriff. I can prove that woman scratched me. All you got to do is ride down there and ask."

Carberry spat the word, "Liar!"

The other man spoke now. "He's telling the truth, Sheriff. The storekeeper never came face to face with him. I paid for the stuff we bought. He's telling the truth about how he got scratched, too."

Horsley said, "All right. Saddle your horses and mount up."

"You're going to take us in? We ain't *done* nothing, Sheriff. Why do we got to go to jail?"

"Shut up and do what you're told. This man's daughter was killed tonight. You're the only strangers around."

The man breathed, "Oh, Jesus!" He and the other man went to their horses, pulled the picket pins and coiled up the picket ropes. They threw on blankets and saddles and then rolled up their bedrolls and gear and tied them behind their saddles. All this time, Carberry was silent, which surprised Horsley until he looked at Carberry's face. Carberry hadn't given up. Horsley decided the only reason he was keeping still was that there wasn't anything for miles from which to hang the men.

The two drifters mounted. Carberry said, beneath his breath, "Go ahead, you sonsabitches! Just try to get away!"

Horsley said, "Give me your reins." He rode close to first one man and then the other, taking the reins of their horses. Leading their mounts, he turned toward town.

Carberry and the other men came along behind. Horsley could hear Carberry talking to them, but they were fifty feet or so behind and he couldn't hear what Carberry said. He had an idea, though. Carberry was trying to stir up the other men.

The return trip to town seemed to take a lot longer than had the trip coming out. They reached town about 3 A.M., and Horsley took his prisoners straight to the jail. They waited meekly while he opened the door and lit the lamp. They walked back to one of the cells. Horsley locked them in.

Carberry had come into the office along with several of the other men. Horsley said, "Go on home, Mr. Carberry. Get some sleep. Tomorrow's soon enough for anything else that needs to be done."

Carberry went out, surprisingly without argument. The others followed him. But Carberry did not go home and neither did the other men. They led their horses across the street and tied them to the rail in front of the saloon where the two cowhands' horses still were tied. They trooped inside.

Briefly, Horsley considered closing the saloon. He decided against it because it would bring on a confrontation with Carberry and with the others who supported him. If they refused to leave there would be little he could do, and he would have lost face and a good bit of his authority, authority he had a feeling he was going to need before this night was over with.

He went back to the cell holding the two men. He said, "I hope to God you two are telling me the truth."

"We are, Sheriff. Honest to God we are. We wouldn't hurt no woman, let alone a girl."

"How'd you know it was a girl? Nobody said it was a girl."

The man's face was gray. "Sure you did. You said that man's daughter had been killed."

"His daughter could've been forty years old, for all you know. But you said 'girl.'"

The man said wearily, "You got us guilty no matter what we say, don't you?" He went to the back of the cell and sat down with the other man on the cot.

Horsley returned to his office, closing the door behind, leaving the cell block dark. He heard the two talking together, but their voices were only a low murmur because of the closed door and he couldn't make out what was being said. He went to the window and stared at the saloon across the street. There were more horses tied there than on Saturday night.

He could imagine what was going on inside. Drinking. Talking. Working up to something, egged on by Carberry. By the time an hour had passed every man in the saloon would have tried and convicted the two strangers in his mind. All that would remain would be executing them.

Yet he could not really believe that would happen. Not in Broken Butte. They'd talk but it would end with talk. They'd go home after a couple of hours and sleep it off and tomorrow they'd have cooled down and forgotten all the big talk of the night before.

He packed and lighted his pipe, noticing how his hands trembled as he did. Irritably, he got up and began pacing back and forth. He could still hear the murmur of voices from the cells. And he could hear another sound—loud voices from across the street.

He crossed the room to where his rifle and a double-barreled shotgun leaned in a corner. He picked up the shotgun and carried it to his desk. He hesitated a moment, started across the room to replace it in the corner, then changed his mind. Instead, he opened one of his desk drawers and took out a handful of cartridges. He glanced at the end of one, noting that it was loaded with OO Buck. He didn't load the gun but neither did he replace the cartridges. He stuffed them into his side pants pocket instead.

He sat down at his desk and put his feet up on its top. He was frowning, thinking how one of the prisoners had said they'd never kill a woman, let alone a girl. Maybe it was a natural thing to say in view of the fact that he himself had said it was Carberry's daughter who had been killed and then again maybe it was a slip of the tongue that betrayed their guilt.

Anyhow, he thought, it didn't have to be decided tonight. Or tomorrow. The judge wouldn't be back for a week or ten days from his circuit. That should provide him with enough time to question the men and investigate the scene of the killing thoroughly and either prove them guilty or innocent.

Strange how quickly Carberry had forgotten about viewing the scene of the killing once the two strangers had been caught. But Horsley knew that an examination of the place could either prove or disprove that the two strangers had been involved. There would be horse and boot tracks. The two cowhands who had found Eloise couldn't have messed up all of them.

The noise across the street increased, and as it did, the murmuring back in the cell died away. The two men were also listening, Horsley thought, probably scared damn near to death.

He fingered the shotgun and realized that he was also scared. He'd never seen a lynching, but he had heard stories told by men who had. He didn't think it possible that his friends and neighbors here in Broken Butte would get worked up enough to lynch the two prisoners, but neither could he entirely discount the possibility. Carberry was an influential man and a persuasive one. A good many of the men in town owed him money. Some were afraid of him. And Horsley had a hunch Carberry was talking lynching over there.

Suddenly, decisively, he took two shotgun shells from his pocket and shoved them into the breech of the gun. He snapped the action shut and laid the gun across his desk. He felt a little foolish, but he also felt comforted. Even if they did come, a double-barreled shotgun would turn them back. He was worrying unnecessarily.

But he couldn't stop worrying. And he couldn't close his ears to the rising sound of voices coming from the saloon across the street.

CHAPTER 5

Over in the saloon, Carberry was, indeed, inciting to violence. He had convinced himself that the two drifting cowboys were guilty of murdering Eloise. Had he examined his own feelings, he would have realized that disillusionment and anger were emotions at least as strong in him as was grief. Eloise, fifteen year old Eloise, the girl who looked so sweet and demure in her photograph had been nothing but a slut with no more morals than an alley cat.

Eloise, hardly more than a child, had lied to him and to her mother so that she could spend the night with a man, or with the two men now in jail accused of killing her.

He didn't want to ask himself the question why. But uneasily in the back of his mind stirred memories of the way Eloise had changed in the last year or so. She had been defiant, disobedient, given to screaming tantrums and bitter accusations against both her father and mother. More than once, Carberry had spanked her and spanked her hard. On at least two occasions, he had swung his open hand in sudden rage at something she had said, leaving an angry red mark on the side of her face that remained for hours but only increased the sullen anger that smoldered in her eyes. Why? For God's sake, why? They'd raised her just about like any of the other parents in Broken Butte had raised their kids.

He gulped his drink, trying to blot these thoughts and

these memories from his mind. He reminded himself angrily that Eloise was dead, killed by the two now lodged in jail. One of them had the marks of her fingernails on his face, put there probably while she fought him for her life.

Around him, the other townsmen gulped drinks quickly as if they feared Carberry would withdraw his order to Sam Flagler to charge all the drinks to him. Had they been paying for their own, they would not have gulped them nearly as fast.

The result was that the liquor took hold of them quickly and Carberry kept fanning their anger with his talk. "What if it'd been your daughter, or your wife? You'd want me to back you up, wouldn't you? Hell yes, you would. Well, by God, I want you to back me up now."

"What do you want us to do?" asked Isodoro Chavez.

For the first time, Carberry faced, in his own mind, what he really wanted the townsmen to do. He wanted the two strangers hanged. He wanted them to pay, tonight, for what they had done to Eloise. He couldn't face waiting until the judge returned, until he got around to holding a formal trial. He couldn't face all the questioning that was sure to take place, and he couldn't face what Eloise had been coming out in open court for all the town to hear. Besides, he didn't have any doubt about the guilt of the two accused. One had scratches on his face, didn't he? And besides, who in town or even on any of the outlying ranches would do such a thing? The answer was that nobody would. So it must have been the two strangers who were now over in the jail.

He yelled, "I say why wait for the judge to come back? Why wait for weeks and maybe even months for those bastards to pay for killing my little girl? They didn't give her any time, did they? They didn't give her any trial. No, sir. They beat her to death with their fists and then left her out there on the prairie like one of her own broken dolls."

The reference to her dolls brought an ominous murmur of anger from the crowd of men. Carberry yelled, "Have one more drink! Then one of you get a couple of ropes and we'll go across the street and get those sonsabitches out of jail. There's that big cottonwood down by the livery barn. We'll string 'em up to it."

There it was, out in the open, put into words at last. Hearing it put so bluntly made the crowd in the saloon go silent, while their minds digested the implications of what Carberry had suggested that they do. But Carberry was the most influential man in town. He was also the wealthiest. He was respected and their judgment had been influenced by the liquor they had consumed, liquor paid for by Carberry himself.

Seward Littlejohn, the town's mortician, who had seen Eloise's battered body when it was brought to his house, yelled angrily, "He's right! There's no damn use waiting weeks to give 'em what's coming to them! They done it. The proof's right on that one bastard's face."

That ugly murmur came again, but there was still some hesitation among a few of them. Littlejohn yelled, "If you all could've seen her like I did you wouldn't be hanging back! It was enough to make a man cry the way she was beat up!"

That did it. The murmur turned to a roar, as every man in the place began to shout. Carberry felt a surge of triumph. The killers were going to pay for what they had done. There would be no need for Eloise's character to be revealed in court. He bawled, "Ropes. A couple of you get ropes. And we'll need two horses. Come on, let's go!"

All of the men had guns. Their horses were tied out in front. By the time they all had gathered in the street, the men who had hurried after ropes were back. They trooped across the street, angry and determined now. One of them beat thunderously on the jail door with the butt of his gun. "Open up, Horsley! We want them two murderers!"

The jail door opened. Horsley stood in it, a double-barreled shotgun in his hands. He took a backward step. The mob surged in and he raised the gun and fired one barrel into the wall above the door. Stone dust sifted down onto their heads. Horsley shouted, "There's another barrel. First one to take a step gets it right in the gut!"

Carberry stood just inside the door. There were two men between him and the sheriff. He yelled, "And then what, Horsley? Your gun'll be empty. How'll you stop us then?"

Horsley didn't reply, but his eyes briefly mirrored his doubt. Carberry gave the man ahead of him a violent shove. The man put his hands against the man in front of him instinctively, pushing that man forward right into the muzzle of the gun. It did not discharge. The man seized the muzzle and shoved it up until the gun was pointing at the ceiling. Still it did not discharge. Horsley, taken by surprise, had not had time to make the decision between protecting his prisoners even at the risk of killing one of his fellow townsmen, or of refusing to shoot into this group of his friends and neighbors. The decision was simply taken out of his hands by Carberry's action in shoving the men ahead of him into the muzzle of Horsley's gun.

They wrenched the gun out of Horsley's hands and pushed him roughly to one side. Horsley yelled at them but he might as well have saved his breath. They stormed into the back, unlocked the cell and dragged the begging, terrified prisoners out.

It was quickly done, so quickly that it horrified the sheriff. Some of the men had lanterns. The others dragged the prisoners toward the livery barn. Horsley went along, yell-ing at them, pleading, trying to make them understand what they were doing.

But the liquor they had consumed and the excitement now had its grip on them. They shoved him angrily aside when he got in their way. They threw the ropes over the horizontal cottonwood branch, and put hangman's nooses in their ends. They boosted the prisoners bodily onto the horses after they had tied their hands behind their backs. A man mounted a third horse and put the nooses over the prisoners' heads. The ends were tied.

Horsley roared, "For God's sake, don't do it! Wait until tomorrow at least! Wait until I've had a chance to go out and look at the place where Eloise was killed!"

"What about the scratches, Sheriff? How you going to explain them away?"

"Maybe what the man said was true. Maybe some saloon girl did put them there."

"Like hell!" roared Carberry. "Get on with it!" He himself gave each horse a cut across the rump with a broken board he had picked up. The horses bolted and the prisoners were yanked out of the saddles and left swinging violently back and forth while their faces grew red, then purple with congested blood. The neck of one had broken and he died quickly, but the one with scratches on his face kicked in violent protest as he slowly choked to death.

Suddenly there was utter silence among the men who had done this thing. The silence was so profound that one man's whisper, "Oh God!" was plainly audible. Another man bolted, and the sound of his vomiting came loudly back to the others.

Horsley felt like vomiting himself. And suddenly the men began slipping silently away as if by so doing they could disassociate themselves from what had just been done.

Horsley watched them go. Then, leaving the two dead

men slowly turning on their ropes, he turned and went back to the jail. He had no intention of cutting the two men down. He'd leave them hang there until somebody else cut them down. He'd tried to stop the hanging and he had failed. Let those who had done it now accept the consequences of what they had done.

He went into his office and sat down. The red sandstone dust and the flattened buckshot pellets on the floor reminded him, if he needed it, of what had happened here tonight.

What should he have done, he asked himself miserably. Could he have stopped the men? By firing into them could he have turned them back?

And supposing he had fired, and had killed Frank Lane, the man in front? Would that have been any better than seeing the two strangers hanged?

Over and over he told himself that it was done, and could not now be changed. Over and over he tried to convince himself that he had done right, that he had done all he could. But the soul sickness did not go away. The deep feeling of guilt did not go away. The memory of those two bodies turning slowly on their ropes remained like a brilliant picture in his thoughts.

The town was quiet now. The men had taken their horses from in front of the saloon and had gone home. The saloon was closed, and dark. The town itself was dark. Half an hour after the hangings, the sheriff's lamp was the only one burning in the town. But he was willing to bet that not a single one of those who had been involved was asleep. Or indeed would be tonight. Liquor and excitement and the prodding of Eric Carberry had made them do what they had done. Now they must live with their guilt just the same as Horsley must.

Horsley opened his bottom desk drawer. He took out a brown bottle. He removed the cork and took a drink. He noticed how his hand shook as he put the bottle down on the top of his desk.

He took another drink and another after that. The liquor could dull his memory of what had happened for tonight. But what about tomorrow and the day after that? What about all the hundreds and thousands of days to come? However he tried to convince himself that he had done all he could, he knew it wasn't true. He was the sheriff and it was his job to protect his prisoners. Whatever the difficulties, he should have done just that. It was his fault that they were hanging down by the livery barn.

Furthermore, he had an uneasy premonition that examination of the place where Eloise Carberry had been killed tomorrow would prove they had been innocent. If that happened, the guilt of the townsmen who had participated would become intolerable. And they would lay the blame on him. Where, indeed, the blame belonged.

CHAPTER 6

Sheriff Horsley woke up on the jail couch in the morning. The empty whiskey bottle lay on the floor beside the couch. He was fully dressed. His head felt like a thousand hammers were beating against the inside of his skull. His mouth was full of cotton. His stomach contracted and he jumped out of bed and ran for the washbasin in the corner of the room.

Afterwards, weak and shaking, he walked to the door, opened it and looked out. From here, he could see one of the bodies, still hanging, still twisting slightly on the rope. He shut the door, feeling his stomach contract again.

At first, upon awaking, he had thought last night had been a nightmare and that he'd find it wasn't true. But it was true. The two strangers were still hanging there for all the town to see.

The door slammed open and Carberry came bursting in. He said, loudly enough to be heard a hundred yards away, "For God's sake, get over there and cut them down!"

Horsley winced. "You cut them down."

Carberry grunted, "Drunken sot!"

Horsley said, "I'm going out to the place where they found your daughter. Do you want to go along? Or are you afraid of what I'll find?"

"I'll go. Now get over there and cut those bodies down."

Horsley suddenly hated him. He looked him straight in the eye. He'd never be elected again anyway so he didn't need Carberry any more. He said, "You go straight to hell, you puffed up son-of-a-bitch!"

Carberry blustered, "You'll be sorry . . ." He didn't finish.

Horsley said, "I am sorry. I'm sorry I didn't blow your head off last night."

Carberry went storming out. Horsley closed the door against the blinding rays of the morning sun. All he wanted to do was go back to bed but he knew he didn't dare. Unless he got out to the scene of Eloise Carberry's murder early this morning, he had a feeling he'd find the tracks messed up. Carberry had committed himself to the belief that the two drifters had murdered Eloise. He didn't want to discover, now, that he had been wrong.

Horsley looked toward the corner where the washbasin was. With a shudder, he put on his hat and went out, closing the door behind him.

Squinting against the glare, he crossed the street to the livery barn. He couldn't see either body after he got halfway across the street. Carberry would get somebody to cut them down. If he was willing to pay enough, he'd get somebody.

Horsley got his horse out of its accustomed stall. He replaced the halter with a bridle, led the animal to the front of the barn and saddled him. He mounted and rode out into the street. The two cowboys who had found Eloise had described the place well enough so that he knew exactly where it was.

He wasn't more than a quarter mile out of town before he heard pounding hoofbeats behind. Turning his head, he saw Carberry's ponderous shape towering over his saddle horse. He waited for Carberry to catch up. In silence, then, the two rode on, reaching the scene of Eloise's death shortly afterward.

Carberry's face was stricken as he stared at the place. Horsley said, "Stay put. I'll look at the tracks."

Carefully and slowly, he rode to the center of the little, brush-surrounded clearing. The scuffed marks of a struggle were plainly evident. So was the impression in the dust made by Eloise's body. Her clothes, or what was left of them, were scattered over a hundred-foot circle. There were the tracks of the two cowboys' horses and their boot tracks around the mark made by Eloise's body. But there was something else, the plain tracks of a buggy and buggy horse.

Seeing that made Horsley's stomach feel empty, made his chest feel hollow and made his spine feel cold. He had been right. The two drifters who had been hanged last night had had nothing to do with Eloise Carberry's death.

He looked toward where Carberry sat impatiently. He called brutally, "You hanged the wrong men, Mr. Carberry. Them two hadn't a damn thing to do with your daughter's death."

Carberry savagely kicked his horse and the animal sprang ahead. Carberry reached the sheriff and swung down to the ground. "What the hell are you talking about?"

Horsley said, "Take a look. Them tracks there are those of the two cowboys who found her and brought her in. There ain't no other horse tracks but those of a buggy horse."

Carberry walked a swift circle, studying the ground. Horsley knelt and studied both the tracks of the buggy wheels and the tracks of the buggy horse. He'd been a lawman for a long time and he read tracks as well as most men could read a printed page. He memorized every feature of each of the horse's four hoofs, as well as every distinguishing feature of each of the buggy wheels. He could find that buggy and buggy horse easily enough in a town the size of Broken Butte. He could find the man who had killed Eloise. But he couldn't restore life to the two drifters they had hanged.

He got back on his horse. He headed for town, leaving Carberry behind, running around like a crazy man trying to find the horse tracks he so desperately wanted to find. He was halfway to town before Carberry caught up with him. Carberry was silent for only a moment and then he said, "Does anybody have to know?"

Horsley looked at him. "Your daughter's killer is right there in Broken Butte. Don't you want to know who he is?"

"Of course I want to know. But can't this all be kept between you and me? I'll see to it that Eloise's killer pays for what he did."

Horsley looked at him. Carberry's true character lay there between them, naked and exposed. Horsley said, "You're as bad as him."

Carberry said, "How'd you like to retire, Horsley? How'd you like to have everything you need for the rest of your life?"

Horsley shook his head. His head still pounded and he felt like throwing up. His hands and knees shook violently. He felt like he was going to die. But he said, as firmly as he could, "I'm going to find the man who killed Eloise. He's going to trial and he's going to be hanged. You've done enough and you're not going to do any more."

Carberry scowled and his slitted eyes were as cold as ice. "You'd better consider that carefully."

Horsley made a thin, humorless grin. "Are you threatening me?"

"Hell yes, I am."

"Who'd you get to cut the bodies down?"

"Gonzales and his son."

"For how much?"

"Ten dollars apiece."

Horsley nodded. Amos Gonzales could use the money but it angered him that Carberry had gotten his dirty job done so cheap. Then he bitterly asked himself what right he had to be angered by Carberry's action. He could have stopped the hanging last night if he'd been resolute enough. Maybe he wouldn't have had to shoot if he'd been willing to and had convinced them that he was. The trouble was he'd let himself believe the two drifters were the guilty ones. Without a trial, without a conviction, he had let himself believe in their guilt which was pretty much what all the other men involved had done.

He made up his mind that he'd leave Broken Butte as soon as the trial was over with. Carberry said, "What are you going to do?"

"What I said I was. Find your daughter's killer and hold him for trial."

Carberry said, "Five thousand dollars."

Horsley hated himself for the instant he let himself consider it. He said, "No."

"And a hundred a month for as long as you live. Just give me the man's name and forget it. He'll be punished."

"What would you do, hire him killed?"

"What's wrong with that? Wouldn't the law hang him?"

"After he was convicted, yes."

"You've mentioned wanting to retire to a ranch someplace. You could go a long ways from here. You'd never have to worry again."

For reply, Horsley dug heels into his horse's sides and the animal thundered away. Carberry stared after him, a scowl on his not-now-genial face. It was going to be the way the sheriff said it was. Nothing he could say or do would change that fact. Unless he had the sheriff killed . . .

He shook his head almost absently, touched his horse's sides with his heels and rode toward town at a trot. He thought of the two drifters, hanged last night for something they hadn't done. He tried to force his thoughts away from them. What the hell did they amount to anyway? What good did they do in the world? They were nothing and he shouldn't let himself think about them. What was done was done.

Horsley found the buggy before he had been in town an hour. It belonged to Ed Cobb. Its iron tires matched the tracks he had found where Eloise Carberry had been killed. Cobb's buggy horse's hoofs matched the tracks left at the scene of the crime.

Cobb was a married man with a three-year-old girl. He worked for Carberry in Carberry's store. It wasn't hard for Horsley to figure out what had happened between Cobb and Eloise. He had been seeing her on the sly. They'd had an all night rendezvous last night. They probably had quarreled and Eloise had threatened to tell her father and Cobb's wife about their relationship. Cobb had known that if she did, his marriage was over, and he would lose his job as well. If there weren't more serious consequences. So in a fit of rage, he had killed her, literally beaten her to death. Then, to make it look like a rape killing, he had ripped off her clothes.

He hadn't planned beyond that. He hadn't taken time to figure out that his tracks would be found and identified.

Horsley arrested him in Carberry's store. He thought Carberry was going to have a stroke when he found out that his own store clerk was the guilty man. He had to threaten Carberry to keep him from attacking Cobb right there in the store.

Carberry tried to stir up the townspeople for another

lynching, but they'd had enough of lynching to last them all their lives.

Cobb went to trial. He pleaded guilty and the judge sentenced him to hang. Horsley refused to preside at the hanging, but he did agree to escort Cobb to Yuma where he was executed shortly afterward. Cobb's wife and child left town and the town tried to forget what had happened.

Maybe eventually they'd have succeeded, if not in forgetting, at least in putting it out of their minds. Now that was going to be impossible. A U. S. Marshal was in Broken Butte to arrest the members of the mob and bring them to trial.

CHAPTER 7

It was dark when Cragg awoke. He was soaked with sweat, but there was a breeze blowing in the open window and out the transom above the door. He laid still a moment, remembering where he was. Then he swung his legs over the side of the bed and sat up.

He got to his feet, stretched and scratched his belly. He walked to the window and stared down into the street. This being a week night, it was almost deserted but the doors of the saloon down the street were open and he could hear the babble of voices inside the place. Several horses stood tied in front of the saloon and one was tied in front of the stage depot. Somewhere in a far part of town a dog barked monotonously.

A peaceful scene, a peaceful-seeming town, except that Cragg knew it was not as serene as it now seemed. Something had happened here in Broken Butte, or something was going to happen, and his presence frightened the townspeople.

He dumped some water into the washbasin and washed. He put on a clean shirt. He got a comb out of his grip, hesitated over his razor, then left it where it was. Hair combed and hat in place, he went out the door and down the stairs.

The big room at the foot of the stairs was deserted. He poked his head into the kitchen, only to find it dark and deserted too. Turning, he saw the station agent standing in the middle of the room watching him.

"Looks like the dining room is closed," he said.

The man nodded. "We don't serve meals regular. Only to the stagecoach passengers."

"Anyplace a man can eat?"

"Easterday's Restaurant is just down the street."

Cragg nodded. He doubted if the restaurant would be open this late but he'd go see. He went out.

The air had cooled somewhat. He felt rested and refreshed. He walked down the street toward the bridge. The restaurant was in the same block as the stage depot. There were lamps burning inside and the door was unlocked. Cragg went in.

A woman came from the kitchen at the rear. At first he thought he knew her, or had known her, and he stood there staring appreciatively at her. She was about thirty-five, with dark, shining hair, a wisp of which had strayed and lay damply across her forehead. A striking woman, with gray eyes that met his own and held them as she said, "I was just about to close."

He nodded. "Excuse me for staring. I thought I had known you somewhere."

That brought a rather strange expression to her face as if she'd had the same feeling when she first saw him. A faint smile touched her mouth. "You're still staring."

He said bluntly, "You're a mighty good-looking woman."

That statement brought a heightened color to her neck and face. She studied him a moment more, silently, then said, "Sit down at the counter. I guess the stew's still warm."

He sat down gratefully. He hadn't wanted to go to bed with an empty stomach and he hadn't fancied the free lunch over at the saloon, over which flies had been crawling when he'd seen it there this afternoon. Before she could leave him and go into the kitchen he said, "I'm Gus Cragg. I came in on the stage this afternoon."

She nodded. "I know." Then, turning, she said, "I'm Clara Easterday."

Gus Cragg had never been one to go at a thing obliquely. He asked, "Where's Mr. Easterday?"

Her glance came back to him, along with the faint smile. She said, "You're a direct man, Mr. Cragg."

He grinned at her. "Saves time. You haven't answered me."

Her smile faded. "Mr. Easterday is dead."

"I'm sorry." He wasn't. He was glad.

"It was a long time ago. Eight years." She let her glance rest on him a moment, disconcertingly, then turned and went into the kitchen. He admired her full-bodied figure openly before she disappeared.

She was gone only a few minutes. When she came back she had a plate of stew, some boiled and buttered potatoes, and some bread that had obviously been baked today. She put the plate down in front of him. "Coffee?"

"Yes, ma'am." He was hungry and he began to eat. She brought him coffee. He glanced up at her between bites. She remained there, watching him. Finally she said, "I like to see a hungry man eat."

"I expect you see it often if all your food's like this."

"You do know how to make a woman feel good, Mr. Cragg."

"It's the truth." He noticed her looking at his badge and said, "I'm a United States Marshal, ma'am. Based in Fort Worth right now."

"Your work must be interesting." A certain strain had come into her voice.

He said, "Mostly it's just hard and tiresome." He changed

the subject deliberately. "This is a real nice town. It gets pretty hot in the afternoon, though."

"It was hot today. It isn't always as hot."

"Have you lived here long?"

She had to think about that for an instant. "About ten years. My husband drove a stagecoach for Butterfield. Apaches killed him and all his passengers one night about eight years ago." The strain was gone now. He felt comfortable with her, and at ease. It was a pleasant feeling, one he rarely had experienced with a woman.

He continued to eat, savoring the food, and they talked casually of a variety of things. He finished and mopped his plate with the last bite of bread. She asked, "Would you like some more?"

He shook his head. Looking up, he saw that her glance had strayed past him and out into the street. Her face had lost color and her eyes had an almost frightened look to them. He turned. Dimly he saw a small group of men standing in the dark street watching him.

He turned and studied her. She pretended there had been nothing unusual in the street.

He asked, "Who are they watching, you or me?"

"Watching? Who?"

He shrugged. "Never mind. It doesn't matter."

She took his dishes and carried them into the kitchen. She was gone for a long time. He turned his head and stared straight at the men in the street, finally forcing them to withdraw from sight.

He wanted to stay. He enjoyed her company. He saw the lamp in the kitchen go out and called, "You wouldn't have another cup of coffee out there would you, Mrs. Easterday?"

She came to the kitchen door. "I thought you were through. I was getting ready to go home."

He didn't say anything and after a moment the ghost of

a smile touched the corners of her mouth. She understood why he had asked for the coffee, her expression plainly saying so. She disappeared, the lamp was lighted again, and after a moment she returned, a cup of steaming coffee in each hand.

She pulled a stool around the end of the counter and sat down facing him. She asked abruptly, "How long are you going to stay in Broken Butte, Mr. Cragg?"

His glance held hers tenaciously. "I haven't decided yet." He'd meant to go out on the stage day after tomorrow, but now he was not so sure. Maybe he'd lay over here a few days more. Clara Easterday was a woman he wanted to get to know.

Her glance went past him and beyond into the street again. He asked, "Are they still out there staring in?"

She nodded.

"What is it about me that interests them?"

"I haven't the slightest idea, Mr. Cragg." But he knew she was lying. She knew why they were watching him. She knew why the town was afraid of him. She knew what the town was trying to hide.

He tried to steer the conversation back to everyday, inconsequential things, without success. She was preoccupied. She kept glancing at his coffee cup to see if it was empty yet. Finally she said, "You are going to have to leave, Mr. Cragg. It is very late."

He nodded. He'd stalled as long as he could. He gulped the rest of his coffee and she took both cups to the kitchen.

Cragg turned his head. The men watching him had become bolder. They had come to this side of the street and were now standing just outside the window staring in. There were three of them. Cragg caught and held their glances, one by one, forcing each man in turn to look away.

But they did not withdraw. Scowling sullenly, they remained, simply refusing to directly meet his glance. He went to the door and opened it. He said, "Is there something I can do for you gentlemen?"

His directness flustered them. One shook his head. Another mumbled something. Cragg spoke with an edge to his voice. "Then suppose you all go home. You're making me edgy and when I get edgy I get curious."

They hesitated, looking at each other. Finally they turned almost in unison and hurried away. He went back into the restaurant, knowing they would not go far. They'd get out of sight but they'd keep watching him.

Clara Easterday stood in the kitchen door. "What did you say to them?"

"I asked them what I could do for them. They didn't have much to say, so I told them they were making me curious. That did it."

He closed the door and put his back to it. "This town is hiding something. What is it, Mrs. Easterday?"

"I don't know what you're talking about." Her voice was angry now. "You've already kept me here away past closing time. Please go so that I can go home."

"I'll find out, one way or another."

"I'd suggest you do just that if you think you can. But stop bothering me!"

He was sorry he had angered her. He regretted the passing of the closeness that had been between them a while ago. He said, "I'm sorry, Mrs. Easterday. I didn't mean to upset you."

"I'm not upset. There is no reason why I should be upset!"

"No, ma'am. Of course not."

Suddenly that small smile was back at the corners of her mouth. She went around the room, blowing out the lamps one by one. She came to the door and he held it for her while she stepped outside. There was a clean, woman smell to her that he found pleasant and stirring too. Glancing up the street he saw the three men silhouetted against light coming faintly from the window of the stage depot.

She locked the door and Cragg said, "Ma'am, let me walk you home."

"No!" It was vehement, unnecessarily so. She started to soften her refusal, then suddenly reversed herself, her eyes on the three men watching them from a ways up the street. "All right," she said defiantly. "Let them see what they can make of this."

She took his arm, her hand firm and strong, and guided him straight up Main toward the watching men.

CHAPTER 8

Clara Easterday walked him up Main, steering him the way a teamster steers his teams and chattering at him all the while as if she had known him for years. He found himself grinning down at her, interjecting an answer to one of her queries here and there, wondering at the sudden change in her. Clara Easterday was not a chattering woman. She was not a woman given to small talk or to talk for talk's sake, yet here she was, running on as if she hadn't a brain in her head. They passed the three watchers and Cragg's grin widened as he thought what their expressions must be. Then they were past. As soon as they were out of the men's hearing, Clara's chatter stopped. She said, "Whew! I haven't talked that fast in years."

He said, "What was it all about?"

"Those three men are trying to scare me and to keep me from talking to you."

"Why would they do that?"

"You really don't know, do you?"

"No, but I'm sure getting curious."

"Don't." She was silent a moment and then she asked, "Why *did* you stay in Broken Butte?"

He replied with a question of his own. "Did you ever ride one of Butterfield's coaches when it was a hundred and thirty degrees inside? I got tired is all. I decided a layover for a couple of days wouldn't hurt."

There was a touch of wonder in her voice. "You're really telling me the truth, aren't you?"

"Sure I am. But that's not what you're telling me. What's this town afraid of? What are they trying to hide?"

They had reached her house. It was built of hand-hewn logs that somebody must have freighted from the mountains to the north. She released his arm and turned to face him and say good night but he spoke before she could. "You made me gulp my coffee a while ago. How about another cup?"

Even in the darkness, he could tell she wasn't looking at him. She was looking past him. The three men must have followed in the hope they'd overhear something. Their continued persistence must have irritated her because she said, "All right, Mr. Cragg. Please come in."

She opened the door and he followed her inside. There were two lamps on the kitchen table and a girl sat there reading a book. Clara Easterday said, "Nan, this is Mr. Cragg. Is there any coffee on the stove?"

The girl appeared to be fourteen or fifteen. Her hair was done in two braids, tied with red ribbon at the ends. She was a girl he would have said was plain until she smiled at him. She said, "I'm afraid it's pretty strong."

Cragg said, "That's all right."

Clara Easterday said, "Please sit down, Mr. Cragg."

He sat down across from Nan. He couldn't see the title of the book. Clara said, "Mr. Cragg came in on the stage today. He's staying over until day after tomorrow."

Nan noticed the badge on Cragg's shirt and her eyes suddenly showed fright. Why she should be afraid, Cragg couldn't guess, but he was getting more curious all the time.

Clara brought him a cup of coffee and one for herself. She sat down next to Nan.

Cragg said, "Those three men who were watching us . . . They're going to think you have told me what the town is trying to hide."

"Let them think whatever they like. I don't care."

"Maybe you *should* tell me. I have a feeling it is something I should know."

She didn't like him pressing her to tell. It showed in her eyes and in the set of her mouth. She said, "It is not my place to tell you anything. Go to Sheriff Horsley and ask him." There was an unexpected sharpness in her voice.

He studied her. Here was a strong woman for all her womanliness, he thought. A woman of character and substance. He wondered why she had not remarried, and knew it could not have been for lack of opportunity. Maybe, he thought, she was waiting for a man who measured up to her first husband and just hadn't found him yet. Cragg wondered how he would measure up.

He also wondered at himself. He had met this woman hardly more than an hour ago and already he was thinking about marriage with her. He scoffed inwardly at himself. If she hadn't found a man she wanted to marry in the eight years she had been widowed, it must mean she was too particular. He wouldn't measure up any better than the others had.

He said, "I'm sorry."

She nodded in acceptance of his apology, but she seemed preoccupied. He finished his coffee, and looked at Nan. "I'm glad I met you, Nan." He got to his feet.

The girl smiled at him. Her mother said, "Bedtime, Nan."

"All right, Mother." She smiled again at Cragg, shyly but in a way that plainly said she liked him, and left the room, carrying one of the lamps. Clara followed Cragg to the door. He opened it and stepped out into the night. She said, "Good-bye Mr. Cragg."

He turned and looked down into her face, in shadow because the light was in back of her. There was no smile on her mouth. Her eyes looked steadily up at him. Bluntly then he asked, "Is anybody courting you, Mrs. Easterday?"

Even with the shadow lying across her face, he could see the color that flooded it. Her lips parted with surprise. Then a smile came to her mouth and her eyes sparkled with amusement. She said, "I'll say this for you, Mr. Cragg, you speak what's on your mind."

"You haven't answered me."

"And I'm not sure I will."

He waited and at last she said, "All right. I'll answer you. Nobody is courting me, Mr. Cragg."

He said, "Somebody is now, Mrs. Easterday. I still have a day and a half in Broken Butte and I mean to make the most of it."

"Good night, Mr. Cragg." She watched him turn and walk away. Only when he had disappeared into the darkness did she go inside and shut the door.

Cragg stopped and stood for a moment less than fifty feet from her door, trying to locate the men who had followed them. He had recognized none of them and was not even sure he had gotten a good enough look to recognize them if he saw them again tomorrow. He heard nothing but now, suddenly, something stirred at the base of his neck. It was a prickling sensation with which he was not unfamiliar.

He scoffed at it, something he didn't often do, because he didn't see how there could be any danger here. They might be interested in his reason for staying over and they might have something to hide, but that didn't mean they meant him any harm.

The street was very dark. A lamp glowed faintly here and there in the window of a house. At the lower end of

Main the lights in the saloon cast a glow on the boardwalk and street in front of its windows and open door. Cragg reached for his pipe and tobacco. Standing there, listening intently, he packed the pipe. He struck a match with a fingernail and held the flame to the pipe bowl while he puffed enough to get it going well.

He blew out the match, now hearing a faint scuffing noise behind him. The prickling at the base of his neck spread downward along his spine. He knew with sudden dismay that he had made a mistake ignoring it. He had made another mistake lighting a match, letting its flame blind him however momentarily.

He heard the scuffing again, this time more plainly, its sound becoming louder as whoever made it rushed at him. He started to whirl, pipe still clenched between his teeth. He saw a shadowy figure closing rapidly with him, and saw something thick and long, like a club, descending toward him.

It had been meant to strike his head, and would have killed him instantly if it had struck where it was aimed. But because he had heard, and because he had whirled, it missed its intended mark and struck him on the shoulder instead.

The force of the blow sent him reeling and knocked the pipe out of his mouth. It struck the ground, scattering sparks. Cragg's shoulder felt as if the blow had broken it. He fell, throwing out his hands automatically to break his fall. One arm, the one whose shoulder had been struck, would not support his weight and collapsed, to dump his face down into the dust of the street.

He tried to roll, tried to get his gun, but his right arm was numb and wouldn't do what he willed it to. The pain in his shoulder was excruciating and bright lights danced before his eyes.

If he had expected them to strike that one blow and run he was wrong. They were on him like wolves on a downed and crippled deer. Frantically they kicked and frantically struck at him again and again with that terrible club, which he knew now was an oaken singletree. One blow glanced off his head, making his head explode with pain. Another struck the same shoulder it had struck before, bringing pain as bad as anything he had ever experienced. He kept rolling, kept trying to get his hands and knees under him. He kept trying to get a hand on his gun. He knew, with shocked horror, that they meant to kill him, meant to beat him to death right here, however unbelievable that might seem.

He couldn't get his gun and he couldn't fight back so he did the only thing left to him. A roar, a wordless shout of desperation and pain came from his lips. It rolled down the street, its urgency and desperation unmistakable to every ear it reached.

The club continued to fall, more frantically now than before if that was possible. Cragg heard voices, excited men's voices, urging speed, urging the club wielder to kill and get it over with.

Desperately he seized the club as it struck him on the hip. One hand was numb, but the other held the club with tenacious desperation until a voice yelled, "The son-of-a-bitch has got hold of the club. Shoot him and let's get this over with!"

Before Cragg's fading senses, before his dust-filled and nearly blind eyes, a light suddenly appeared, one that weaved back and forth, growing larger and brighter all the time. Another voice filled his ears, this one the screaming voice of a woman. He felt as if he was falling, through black and endless space, but he held onto the singletree as if his life depended on his doing so, which probably it did. One more blow to the head would have ended it for him.

A gun flared. The bullet hit the ground and sprayed dirt into his eyes.

More screaming, more shouting. The light was closer, almost on top of him. The men's voices faded and were gone. The light was blinding now.

Again he heard the woman's voice, no longer screaming. He felt a woman's hands, and heard her ask, "Are you badly hurt, Mr. Cragg? Should I get the doctor or do you think you can walk?"

He mumbled something and tried desperately to come to his hands and knees. With her help he made it. He steadied himself until the world stopped reeling before his eyes, until the flashing bright lights stopped whirling and began to dim. Clara Easterday said, "Mr. Cragg! Are you all right?"

He mumbled something from between smashed and swollen lips. It was meant to be, "Hell yes, I'm all right," but it only came out as something she could not understand. She asked, "Do you think that you can stand?"

He put forth another monstrous effort and, with her help, made it to his feet. Automatically he felt his holster for his gun. It was gone. He stood there swaying and croaked, "My gun! Find my gun."

Clara said, "Hold him up, Nan, while I try to find his gun."

Other hands took hold of him on the other side. The lantern waved back and forth a few times and finally Clara Easterday's voice said, "Here it is." He felt it returned to its holster. Clara's hands took hold of him on the right side. He felt like crying out from the pain but he clenched his teeth and made no sound. Slowly, painfully, the trio inched back toward Clara's log house, toward the square of light that marked its open door.

Cragg stumbled and went to hands and knees, pulling both of them down with him. Laboriously, once more, they lifted him and continued toward the door. He stumbled again and sprawled forward on the parlor floor. This time they did not try to lift him, but only moved his legs enough so that they could close the door.

Clara said, "Get me a pan of hot water and some clean cloths. And get that brown bottle of whiskey out of the pantry."

Then Clara was kneeling at his side and her pleasant, woman fragrance was in his nostrils, her hands gently exploring his head in an attempt to discover how badly he was hurt.

Cragg closed his eyes. He knew Clara Easterday had saved his life. What he didn't know was why anyone here in this strange town should want him dead.

CHAPTER 9

Clara Easterday was terrified to realize that the men of Broken Butte had actually tried to kill August Cragg. His head was battered and it was a wonder his shoulder wasn't broken. One ear was nearly torn loose from his head. His clothes were splattered with blood and he was a mass of bruises and welts. Only her appearance on the scene had saved his life.

She sponged off his face and explored the bumps on his head with her fingers to see if the skin had been badly cut. He had been stunned and close to unconsciousness at first, but his eyes were clearing now. He took the brown bottle of whiskey out of her hand, pulled the cork and took a drink. He said hoarsely, "They meant business."

"It certainly looks that way." Despite her worry over the close call he had had, a curtain was already coming down over her eyes and he saw she had no intention of telling him what it was all about. She was wrong, of course, but she thought she was doing right. She probably figured that the less he knew the better his chances of leaving Broken Butte alive would be.

Gus Cragg was used to danger. Every time he went on an assignment he lived with it. Even accompanying a prisoner from Fort Apache to Fort Worth was dangerous because the instant he closed his eyes his prisoner would try killing him.

But this was different. He didn't know what he was up

against or who his enemies were. He didn't know what they were trying to keep from him. He said, "It's going to be better for everyone concerned if you just tell me what they're trying to hide."

"I can't do that."

"Then you admit you know?"

"I know. Everybody in town knows."

"And it's so serious they're willing to kill me to keep me from finding out?"

"Maybe they weren't trying to kill you. Maybe they only wanted to scare you into leaving town." But her tone held no conviction.

He said, "I can't leave town. Not until the stage comes through day after tomorrow."

"You could hire a horse. Or a rig."

"I could, but I'm not going to. I think I'm going to stay and find out what's going on. I have a feeling it's something I ought to know."

She had finished her examination of his head. "You're as stubborn as you are hardheaded." There was exasperation in her voice.

He turned his head, winced, and grinned at her. "Maybe. But I know you saved my life."

"Nonsense. They wouldn't have killed you."

He knew that wasn't true and so did she. He put his hands on the table and pushed himself to his feet. "I'm a danger to you." He looked at Nan. Her face was white and her eyes were scared. He said, "I won't see either of you again until I find out what's going on."

Nan said, "Tell him, Mother. He ought to know."

Cragg shook his head. "No. I'd rather find out from somebody else."

He walked to the door, feeling unsteady but trying not to stagger or show his dizziness. He looked at Clara for a long moment, trying to read her glance. Then he stepped out into the night, pulling the door closed behind him.

He waited there for an instant until his eyes became accustomed to the lack of light. Moving away, he dropped a hand to the grips of his gun and let it stay there. The townspeople weren't going to attack him again with impunity. Next time, one or more of them were going to get hurt. Next time he'd be ready and would use his gun.

He moved out into the middle of the street so that he couldn't be surprised. He walked toward the light coming from the windows of the saloon.

He couldn't see them and he couldn't hear them, but he knew that they were there. He wondered if one of them would shoot him from the darkness and admitted it was a possibility. But not until the light was better. Not until they could be sure of hitting him.

One lamp burned in the stage depot. He stepped quickly inside, and quickly stepped to one side so that he would not be silhouetted against the light. Kubec, the man who ran the stage depot, was not in the room. But there was a man sitting on the far side of it, smoking a cigar. Cragg crossed to him.

The man stood up. He was as big as Cragg, but paunchier. There was an easy, genial smile on his blunt-featured face. A homely man, his face was seamed with geniality and yet there was something in his eyes that was not genial at all. He extended his hand. "Mr. Cragg? I'm Eric Carberry."

Cragg looked at the hand a moment, then put out his own. Carberry's grip was exactly right, not limp, not overly strong. He was neither weak, nor did he feel compelled to prove anything. He stared at Cragg's battered face. "What happened to you?"

Cragg said, "I guess somebody thought my wallet was fatter than it really is."

"That's terrible! Have you reported it to the sheriff?"

"Not yet. Did you want to see me about something, Mr. Carberry?"

"Yes. I was wondering how long you plan to stay in Broken Butte."

"Why? What difference does it make?"

"Not many strangers come to Broken Butte. You can't blame us for being curious."

"I plan to stay over until the next stage comes through. I might stay longer if anything more happens to stir my curiosity."

"What do you mean?"

"I mean that the men who attacked me weren't after my wallet. They tried to kill me and they damn near succeeded." Cragg realized that he didn't like Carberry. The man showed the world a front of geniality but underneath he was as cold and ruthless as a grizzly bear. In every town there was a man who ran things and Carberry must be the one who ran things in Broken Butte.

Carberry said, "I'll see that the attack is reported to the sheriff."

Cragg said wearily, "Why? Are you the one that runs this town? Were the men who attacked me following your orders? What I want to know is why you're so interested in me. What are you afraid of, Mr. Carberry?"

Carberry's eyes were glittering. "I'm not afraid of anything, Mr. Cragg."

"Then why do you want to be rid of me?"

Studying Carberry, Cragg could see he was getting under the big man's skin. He felt a gleeful satisfaction that he was because his head ached abominably and he hurt all over from the beating he'd sustained. He suspected Carberry was behind the attack on him and he wanted to make him admit he was.

Carberry said as grimly, "I don't want to be rid of you. And I would suggest, Mr. Cragg, that you make yourself less objectionable in Broken Butte while you are staying here, or I will get in touch with your superiors."

Cragg grinned widely now. A little more, he thought. A little more. He said, "Would you like me to go to the telegraph office with you, Mr. Carberry? I wouldn't want you to send your complaint to the wrong people."

The smile had faded entirely from Carberry's face. His eyes were narrowed with fury. He said, "Damn it, Cragg, I'll . . ."

"You'll what, Mr. Carberry?"

Carberry's fists were clenched. He was tense, holding himself under control with obvious difficulty. Cragg, still grinning, said, "What happened here in Broken Butte? What are you so damned anxious to keep from me? Did you have a lynching, Mr. Carberry?"

He pulled the word "lynching" out of the air, but even as he said it, he knew how logical it was. The whole town knew what they wanted kept from him. A lynching was the only thing it could be.

The word seemed to act as a trigger to Carberry. He lurched forward, seizing Cragg's throat with both his big and powerful hands. Cragg was carried backward by the force of Carberry's attack.

He felt himself falling and carried Carberry with him by seizing the man's wrists with both his hands. The pair crashed to the floor, shaking the building with their combined weight.

Cragg realized, even as he fought for air, even as he tried to tear Carberry's hands from his throat, how much he welcomed this. It was a way to retaliate against the faceless ones who had attacked and tried to kill him earlier. Carberry had probably ordered the attack. Now let Carberry pay the bill.

He brought a knee up with savage satisfaction into Carberry's groin. The man grunted with pain and his hands relaxed enough for Cragg to tear them free. As he rolled, he saw men crowding in the front door, spreading to either side so that they could watch.

He had made a mistake in taunting Carberry into attacking him. If it looked like he was going to win, the others would enter the fight and this time they'd succeed in killing him because there would be no Clara Easterday to intervene. Or maybe they all wouldn't enter the fight. It was impossible that the whole population of the town had participated in the lynching. There must have been some who had protested and even more who had stayed out of it.

Carberry kicked out at him as he came to his hands and knees. The man's foot caught him on the side of the jaw, stunning him, knocking him flat once more. Carberry came scrambling after him, but Cragg stayed away long enough to come erect. Carberry came up too, and rushed at Cragg using his head as a battering ram.

Cragg sidestepped to avoid the rush. But as Carberry went past, he seized the man's belt and collar. Holding Carberry erect, running alongside him, he carried Carberry straight across the room and into the wall with a crash that shook the building once more, this time with enough force to bring dishes clattering from their shelves in the kitchen.

Carberry collapsed and lay without moving. Cragg thought, "He'll have a headache like mine tomorrow, the son-of-a-bitch!"

But Carberry had a harder head than Cragg had supposed. Groaning, he stirred and tried to make it to his hands and knees. Cragg watched him out of one corner of his eye, watched the crowd of men out of the other. He had the upper hand right now and he meant to keep it. The minute he lost it they'd move in for the kill.

There was light and he recognized some of them. Kubec was there and so were a couple he had seen in the saloon yesterday. The saloonkeeper, Sam Flagler, was there and there were several others he had never seen before.

Carberry regained sufficient consciousness to try and reach out for Gus Cragg's legs. He stepped out of Carberry's reach. He stared at the men standing just inside the door. "How many of you were in on the lynching you're trying so damned hard to hide?"

None of them answered him. Cragg said, "It's light in here. How many of those who tried to kill me a while ago have got the guts to step forward and try it again here in the light?"

Nobody came forward. Cragg said sourly, "I thought so. Mobs operate best in the dark." His voice turned brittle with contempt. "Get out of here before I arrest the bunch of you and take you down to the jail."

There was little hesitation after that. They turned and disappeared through the doorway as quickly as they could. Cragg glared at Carberry. The big man was sitting up. He was only half conscious, and didn't seem to know what had happened to him.

Angrily, but with some satisfaction, Cragg turned away from him and headed for the stairs. He knew their secret now. But because he did, he knew his life wasn't worth very much.

CHAPTER 10

Sheriff Horsley heard the shot. Sleeping, it woke him, and he lay there in the darkness for a moment, listening. He knew he ought to get up and investigate, but he lay still, telling himself that if he heard a second shot he would get up. Someone might have discharged a gun accidentally, but a repetition would rule out that theory.

The shot was not repeated. He thought he heard a shout, though, and stayed completely still, waiting for a repetition of the shout. It didn't come.

Horsley knew that something was going on. He knew it was his duty to get up and find out what it was. But he didn't want to know. If he didn't get up, if he didn't investigate, then he wouldn't have any difficult decisions to make. He closed his eyes and tried to go back to sleep but he could not. His ears were tuned to each small sound. He thought he heard men's voices but admitted he could have been mistaken about that.

Not that voices at this time of night would be unusual enough to merit investigation. The saloon was still open. Probably, he told himself, somebody'd had too much to drink and had fired off a gun in drunken exuberance. He had shouted afterward. There was nothing more to it than that.

How long he lay there he could not have said. It must have been half an hour at least. A pounding on the door made him swing his legs over the side of the cot. He reached for his pants and pulled them on. The knocking sounded again, more urgently this time, and he called, "I'm coming! I'm coming! Hold your horses, will you?"

He buttoned his pants and put on his shirt. Barefooted he went to the door.

Clara Easterday was standing there. She said, "I want to talk to you."

"Sure. But can't it wait until morning?"

"No it can't. I want to talk to you right now."

"All right," he muttered resignedly and turned. He lighted the lamp on his desk. He grunted, "You might as well sit down."

She was staring at him suspiciously. "Didn't you hear anything a while ago?"

"Like what?"

"A gunshot. Didn't you hear it?"

"No I didn't," he lied. "What happened? Did somebody get shot?"

"Somebody got shot at." Her voice was filled with angry exasperation. She plainly didn't believe his statement that he hadn't heard the shot.

"Who? Is he badly hurt?"

"Would you care if he was?"

Horsley looked at her with exaggerated patience. "Would you mind telling me what you're talking about?"

"All right. Some men tried to kill Marshal Cragg about half an hour ago. They almost made it, too. If I hadn't come running with a lantern and scared them off, they'd have finished him."

"Who fired the shot? Did he shoot one of them?"

"No. One of them shot at him."

"And missed?"

"Yes."

"I'm glad to hear it. We sure don't need a U. S. Marshal getting murdered here."

"No we don't, do we? We've got enough on our consciences, haven't we?"

"That's over with. It's time we tried forgetting it."

"Those men who tried to kill the marshal weren't forgetting it. They thought he knew what had happened here in Broken Butte."

"Didn't he?"

"No he didn't. He just got tired of the heat inside the stage. He was worn out from being bounced around. He wanted to rest for a couple of days."

"And that was all there was? Are you sure?"

"Of course I'm sure. He's been trying to get me to tell him what the people here are trying to hide, but I wouldn't tell."

Horsley said, "Oh for God's sake."

Clara Easterday studied him impatiently. "Don't you think it's time you started acting like a sheriff for a change? If that marshal gets killed here in Broken Butte it won't be two weeks before there's a swarm of them in here."

"Yes ma'am. You go on home. I'll see what I can do."

She stared at him suspiciously for several moments. Then, with a shrug of resignation, she turned and went out the door.

He waited until she had been gone several minutes. Then he pulled on his socks and boots, put on his hat and buckled on his gun. He blew out the lamp and went outside.

The saloon was still open and there were six or seven men inside. He poked his head in the door. "Anybody seen Carberry?"

One of the men said, "Last I seen him he was over at the stage depot. That marshal ran him into the wall and damn near killed him."

Horsley suspected at least some of them had had something to do with the attack on Cragg but he had no proof and besides he knew if they had, Carberry had given them the idea. He crossed the street and went into the stage depot. Kubec was there but Carberry wasn't. Horsley said, "Where's Carberry?"

"He went home."

"How long ago?"

"Ten minutes, I guess. He didn't feel so good."

Horsley didn't comment on that. He walked up the street toward Carberry's house. There was a light in the kitchen so he went around the back. He could see Carberry sitting at the kitchen table, alone, a bottle and glass in front of him. He knocked.

Carberry opened the door. "Oh, it's you."

"Yes it's me." Horsley went in without being invited. He looked sourly at the bottle and then at Carberry, who was scowling angrily at him. "Got another glass?"

Carberry sullenly got a glass and Horsley poured himself a drink. He poured another and downed that too, and then he said contemptuously, "You stupid fool!"

Carberry's face lost color. "Don't you talk to me like that!"

Horsley said, "Shut up and listen for a change! He didn't know. He laid over because he was worn out by the heat and the jolting of the coach. But he knows now. Or if he don't, he will."

"Does he know, or don't he?"

"I don't know."

"That stupid woman—Clara Easterday—if she'd kept her damned mouth shut . . ."

"She did keep her mouth shut. She hasn't told him anything. It's that try at killing him that's got him wondering. And that's your doing."

"I don't know what you're talking about."

"You're a liar. They didn't get the idea of killing Cragg all by themselves. Any more than they got the idea of lynching those two drifters."

"I don't have to sit here and listen to this. Get out of here. And you can get rid of any notions you've got about being re-elected sheriff in this county again."

Horsley said disgustedly, "Don't threaten me. I wouldn't stay on as sheriff if it paid ten times what it does. You take the sheriff's job. You want to run everything, run the sheriff's office too. But you'd better do a smarter job of it than you've been doing with everything else."

Carberry said stubbornly, "He knew. He came here to investigate. Somebody wrote the government about those two drifters that were hanged."

Horsley shook his head. "He was just passing through."

Carberry was scowling. He poured himself another drink and downed it at a gulp. "All right. But he asked me if we'd had a lynching here."

"He was guessing. He only knows we've got something to hide that he ought to know about. He knows it's serious enough so that we're willing to kill a U. S. Marshal to keep it hidden."

"You think he's going to stay and investigate?"

"If I was him, I would."

Carberry made a contemptuous snort, and Horsley's face darkened. He said, "I hope he finds out what we did. I hope he brings in help and I hope he brings every member of your lynch mob to trial."

"That's big talk for a man that gave his prisoners to the mob."

"Giving up my prisoners wasn't a crime. Lynching is."

"Then we've got to get rid of him. If he wasn't sent here

to investigate the lynching, then nobody knows he's here. If he disappears, nobody will know where he disappeared."

"The people that live here will."

"Not if they don't know that what happened to him happened here."

"McBee, the stage driver will."

Carberry thought about that for a moment. Then he said, "Not if something was to happen to McBee."

Horsley stared at him in disbelief. "You'd kill two men to keep those hangings from coming out?"

Carberry returned his stare impatiently. "Why not? There were nine men in that lynch mob besides me. They're all good men. They made one mistake, that's all. Do you think they ought to go to Yuma for ten years or more just because of one mistake? You know what Yuma's like. It would be the same as killing them. Looks to me like two lives are a pretty cheap price to pay for ten."

Horsley said drily, "Particularly if one of the two lives isn't yours."

"No need to get sarcastic. I'm just being practical. We don't know this marshal."

"We know McBee."

"All right, so we know McBee. But he doesn't live in Broken Butte."

"And that makes his life worth less. Is that what you're trying to say?"

Carberry stared at him angrily. "No, that isn't what I'm trying to say. I know killing the marshal is wrong. I know killing McBee is wrong. What I'm trying to do is be practical. The lives of ten men are at stake. Ten good men."

Horsley said bitterly, "Nine."

"All right, exclude me if you want." There was desperation in that admission coming from Carberry. "Nine good men. You were in the war. You know that lots of times a few men were sacrificed for the good of many. It happened all the time."

Horsley asked, "And who is the executioner going to be?"

Carberry said, "You wouldn't be sorry, Horsley. I can promise you, you wouldn't be sorry."

Horsley said, "You can go to hell. I'm not going to do your dirty work for you. And furthermore, I'm going to stop you. I may even tell that marshal what he's up against so he can telegraph for help."

Carberry's voice was soft. "I wouldn't do that, if I were you."

Horsley uttered a single, savage obscenity. He went to the door, stepped out into the night and slammed the door thunderously behind him. Furiously he strode toward his office at the lower end of Main.

CHAPTER 11

As he passed the saloon, Horsley could see men inside, but there was little noise coming out the open doors. He saw a few men outside the place, either silent men or men talking in lowered tones. He went into his office and lighted the lamp. He stood for a moment in the open doorway, staring into the street, before he turned and sat down at his desk.

Carberry had proposed the cold-blooded murder of two men and had, furthermore, had the gall to suggest that Horsley commit the murders for him. Well, to hell with Carberry. He had run the town to suit himself for years and people were used to doing what he told them to. But that didn't mean they had to do everything he told them to.

This time it was going to be different. Horsley had no intention of being involved in two more killings. As it stood now, nobody could hold him criminally responsible just because he'd let armed men take his prisoners away from him.

On the other hand Carberry and the nine others who had actually hanged the men knew they could go to Yuma Prison for what they had done. Horsley couldn't really blame them for trying to keep what had happened from being known. It *had* been a mistake and they *had* been egged on by Carberry. They had let themselves be egged on because they were used to doing what Carberry told them to. But to murder two men in cold blood now to keep their guilt from being known . . . Angrily Horsley shook his head. He got to his feet and began to pace nervously back and forth.

He glanced at his office clock. It was eleven-thirty. Ordinarily the saloon would be almost empty at this time of night. He stopped at the open door and stared into the street.

He didn't know August Cragg, he told himself. The man meant nothing to him. But that was no justification for turning his head the other way while Carberry and those willing to help him disposed of Cragg.

And he did know McBee. He knew him well and liked him. It had been hard living with the fact that he'd let the mob have his two prisoners but if he looked the other way now and let McBee be killed he'd never be able to live with it.

Or would he? Didn't time make things easier to bear? When he'd lost his wife ten years ago he hadn't thought he'd be able to endure the grief, the emptiness and loss. He'd thought the loneliness would be unendurable. But time *had* made it endurable. He missed his wife even to this day but it didn't obsess his thoughts day and night. He lived and was content and sometimes weeks went by without even the thought of her crossing his mind.

It would eventually be the same with respect to the two prisoners he had given up to the mob. And if Cragg and McBee were killed, perhaps he could eventually learn to live with that.

Sourly he examined himself and he didn't like what he saw. Murder begets murder, he thought, and crime begets crime. Each one steals from a man more of his principles and more of his manhood until at the last there is nothing left.

But what was he going to do? Could he expose ten of his fellow townsmen, most of whom he liked, to Cragg? Could he be responsible for sending them to Yuma Prison, to that boiling hell on earth? He realized that he was soaked with sweat. He crossed the room and stood in front of the door. A small breeze came in, warm but still a breeze. It cooled his soaked body but it couldn't ease his tortured thoughts.

He *knew* what he ought to do. He was the sheriff, the guardian of the law. The fact that he'd made one mistake didn't justify making more. So far, he wasn't guilty of any crime. But if he permitted the murder of Cragg and McBee, he would be as guilty as the men who actually committed the crimes.

It was his duty to seek Cragg out immediately. It was his duty to tell him the whole story, sparing none of the shameful details. But he knew that he wouldn't. At least not yet. Carberry wouldn't kill Cragg himself, and maybe he wouldn't be able to get anybody else.

Even as he had the thought he knew it wasn't true. An attempt had already been made upon Gus Cragg's life. Except for chance, the man would now be dead.

But wouldn't he now be on guard? Of course he would. It wasn't going to be easy to kill a man with the marshal's background if he was on guard.

No, he wouldn't tell Cragg just yet. As long as Cragg knew his danger, he could probably take care of himself. And McBee wasn't due back until the day after tomorrow, so he'd be in no danger until then.

Maybe the marshal would just get on the stage and forget what had happened here. Maybe he'd decide it had only been an attempted robbery.

Maybe. Maybe. Savagely Horsley kicked out at the desk and then scowled when he hurt his foot.

He remembered Cragg's face, his eyes. He imagined the look that would come over the marshal's face when he found out that Horsley had surrendered two innocent prisoners to a mob. Then he knew that Cragg's contempt for him could be no greater than his contempt for himself.

Maybe he'd have to tell Cragg everything before this was over with. But he could delay it for a while. He'd put it off just as long as he could.

Gus Cragg sat in his dark room for a long time. They hadn't had to tell him what the town's secret was. He had surmised and he knew now that his guess had been correct. There had been a lynching in Broken Butte. Furthermore, the men lynched must have been innocent or the townsmen wouldn't be trying so desperately to hide what they had done.

The question was, what was he going to do about it? He had an assignment. He was supposed to pick up a prisoner at Fort Apache and return him to Fort Worth. On the other hand, he realized that he couldn't ignore what had happened here in Broken Butte. Nor did he feel like ignoring an attempt to take his life.

What he ought to do, he supposed, was to get out of town, by horseback or by hired rig, immediately. He could come back later with some deputies and get to the bottom of the lynching. Only he had a feeling they wouldn't let him get out of town. They'd follow him, or they'd gun him down as he tried to leave.

Nor could he simply stay until the next stage. They'd tried to kill him once and they would try again. They were desperate and therefore doubly dangerous.

The normal thing to do would be to confront the local sheriff with what he suspected and also with the fact that there had been an attempt on his life. By watching the sheriff's face, he was pretty sure he would know whether his guess that there had been a lynching here was correct, and also whether the sheriff had been in on the attempt against his life.

He put on his hat and went out of the room. He didn't lock it but simply closed the door. He went down the stairs. The clock in the lobby said it was eleven forty-five.

Kubec sat in a chair, his feet stretched out in front of him reading a newspaper. He glanced over the top of it at Cragg, then glanced back down again. Cragg didn't speak. He stepped out into the night.

He was sweating. The night air wasn't cool by any means but there was a slight breeze blowing and this had a cooling effect as it evaporated the perspiration. Cragg stood there several moments, studying the street, its shadows and the saloon, whose doors were open and from which issued the sound of voices.

The sheriff's office adjoined the two-story courthouse which was in the middle of the next block down, on the same side of the street as the stage depot. There also was a light in it.

Cragg slowly walked that way. The weight of his holstered revolver was comforting against his side. They wouldn't take him by surprise again. And if they tried, somebody was going to be damned sorry because he intended to use his gun.

He reached the sheriff's office without incident and stepped inside. Sheriff Horsley was sitting at his desk. He glanced up almost guiltily as Cragg came in the door. Cragg said, "Evenin', Sheriff."

"Evening, Marshal. What can I do for you?" Horsley was looking at the damage done to Cragg's face during the attack.

Cragg said, "You can answer some questions. You can tell me, for instance, why I was attacked and damn near killed a while ago and why you didn't even come to see if I knew who was behind the attack."

Horsley tried to look surprised. "Attacked? In Broken Butte? I can't believe it."

Cragg said sourly, "I didn't fall down the stairs."

"Who would do such a thing? This is a peaceful town, Marshal. I can't imagine . . ."

Cragg said, "You're a liar. You know I was attacked and you likely know who did it, too. Furthermore, you know why they tried killing me."

"That's crazy, Marshal. Why would anybody here want to kill you? They don't even know you."

"Then it's got to be because of the badge, doesn't it? And that adds up to just one thing. This town has got something to hide, something they think I came here to investigate."

Horsley tried and failed to meet the marshal's glance. Cragg said, "All right, then let me guess what it is. Somebody was lynched here in Broken Butte and it turned out later he was innocent. Now everybody that participated is afraid I'm going to find out who they are. They're afraid of an investigation and they're afraid of going to trial."

Horsley gave him a sickly grin. "You got one hell of an imagination, I'll say that for you."

Cragg suddenly made up his mind. He wouldn't leave day after tomorrow on the stage. He would stay here and get to the bottom of Broken Butte's secret no matter how long it took. The prisoner was safe in the stockade at Fort Apache and there wasn't any immediate urgency about getting him back to Fort Worth.

He said, "Sheriff, you tell your lynch mob that trying to kill me a while ago was the worst mistake they ever made.

You tell them I'm going to stay until I find out what happened here." He smiled grimly. "Tell them, too, that I wasn't sent here to look into it at all. I was on my way to Fort Apache to pick up a prisoner. I just got tired of the heat and the beating I was taking in that coach and decided to rest for a couple of days. Tell them what a bunch of damned fools they made out of themselves."

The sheriff looked as if he was going to be sick. His skin was greenish and his face was shiny with sweat. He stammered, "I still don't know what you're talking about."

Cragg couldn't resist one last vicious dig. "Tell them about Yuma Prison, too, Sheriff. Tell them what it's like down there. Tell them about the graveyard where more prisoners go than ever get released. Tell them how many years a man gets for murder in this Territory."

Horsley didn't speak. Cragg turned and went out. The screen door slammed and Horsley could hear the marshal's boot heels pounding on the boardwalk as he went on up the street toward the stage depot.

Clara Easterday's story had been true. If Carberry had only had the sense to let well enough alone. The marshal would have taken the next stage and that would have been the end of it.

But no. Carberry'd had to instigate an attack on the marshal. He'd had to try getting rid of him. Now the marshal was hurting from the attack, and mad, and determined to find out for sure what was going on.

They would have to kill him now because if they didn't he'd find out exactly what had happened and he'd get the names of all those who had been involved. The Territorial Governor would send in militia and a federal judge. Carberry had influence in Broken Butte County but he had absolutely none outside of it.

He got up and began to pace back and forth again like a

nervous coyote in a cage. He was sweating copiously again.

There was one thing he *could* do now, he thought. He could get a horse at the livery stable, and he could ride away from Broken Butte. He could go to the far end of the county and stay for a couple of weeks. There were things to be done over there, some papers to be served. He'd meant to go next week but he could go tonight instead and by the time he got back, everything would likely be over with.

Longingly he considered it, but even as he did, he knew he couldn't go. It would be the night of the lynching all over again. He'd feel as responsible for the deaths of the marshal and McBee as he now did for the deaths of the two drifters that had been lynched.

No. He'd stay and this time he'd try to do what was expected of him. For the first time, a little core of fear began to grow inside his chest. If he stood in the way of those who wanted Cragg and McBee dead they'd kill him too. Or they would try.

CHAPTER 12

When Clara Easterday left the sheriff's office, she went straight home. She was frightened and disturbed. Nothing like this had ever happened in Broken Butte. There had never been any violence of any kind until the night Eloise Carberry was killed.

Now it seemed to be getting commonplace, and worse, the sheriff didn't appear inclined to try putting a stop to it. Marshal Cragg had been attacked and nearly killed almost outside her door. If she hadn't heard the commotion and come running, he probably would be dead.

She locked her door for the first time in her memory by bolting it. She turned up the lamp, which she had turned down when she left. She poured herself a cup of strong, lukewarm coffee and sat down at the table with it in front of her.

There was no sound in the house. Apparently Nan was fast asleep. She thought briefly that Nan and Eloise Carberry had been the same age. Yet Eloise had been involved with a man and capable of blackmailing him. She wondered briefly if she really knew Nan as well as she thought she did. Probably all parents thought they knew their children but obviously neither Eric Carberry nor his wife had known Eloise.

Impatiently she shook off those disturbing thoughts. There were more urgent things to worry about. She thought of Marshal Gus Cragg, remembering his size, his flat-planed, strong face, his penetrating eyes. He was a man used to violence, she thought. In fact, violence was his life, his livelihood. But it hadn't hardened or soured him. There was kindness in him and something that made her heart beat a little faster when, in her mind, she visualized his face.

He would have to stay here in Broken Butte at least until the day after tomorrow when the stage came through. Then she remembered the viciousness of the attack that had been made on him and remembered his battered face and his shoulder, which would have been broken had he been less powerfully built. He ought, at least, to know what he was up against. He ought to know why the people of Broken Butte were so determined to kill him and he ought to be warned that they would try again.

No one was going to tell him, though, unless she did. Only briefly did she consider the consequences of what she had decided she must do. She would have to leave Broken Butte. Her action would probably result in the sentencing of ten of the men in town to Yuma Territorial Prison, known to be a hell on earth. She would have to leave, and she would lose everything, even her house, because it was certain no one in Broken Butte would buy it from her. Telling Cragg what had happened here might even bring violence down on her and on Nan.

She had never thought of herself as being particularly courageous but she had a strong sense of right and wrong. She turned down the lamp again, discovering that her knees were shaking as she got to her feet. Fleetingly she thought it would be easier if she just blew out the lamp and went to bed but she never seriously considered it. Right was right and what she meant to do was very right. It was just as simple as that.

She unbolted the door and stepped out into the darkness, quickly closing the door and instinctively stepping to one side as she did. They might be watching her and if they were they would certainly guess what she meant to do.

She stood there for several long moments, intently listening. She heard nothing. The air was hot and stifling but there was the faintest breeze blowing and it helped to cool her. She realized suddenly how much she was perspiring but her perspiration was caused only partly by the heat. It was mostly caused by fear.

Walking slowly, silently, and fearfully, she went around the house and along the gravel walk to the street. The grating of the gravel beneath her feet seemed to make a thunderous noise. She reached the walk and started down toward the stage depot.

There was light coming from the open doors of the saloon, casting an oblong pattern on the walk and the street in front of it. There was a glow down where the sheriff's office was which she assumed was light coming from its windows. Overhead the stars were bright and the sky was clear.

A beautiful night. A night that ought to be free of fear. But her legs were still trembling and her chest was filled with a cold ball of terror. She had seen what the townsmen had done to Cragg. She knew they might do the same thing to her.

Unbelievable. And yet it had to be believed despite the fact that she knew each and every member of the mob and also knew their families.

She crossed Maple Street. She reached the place where the attack had been made upon Marshal Cragg. She hurried past, wanting to run but knowing if she did she would only make her situation more precarious.

What would she say if somebody stopped her? She could

say she thought she had left a lamp burning in the restaurant. She could say she had forgotten to kill the fire in the stove. But she knew no story she could tell would be believed. If they didn't attack her the way they had Marshal Cragg they would at least escort her firmly back home again.

Maybe, she thought, she should go back home. At least for tonight. She could tell the marshal about the lynching when she saw him tomorrow.

Except that tomorrow might be too late. He ought to know tonight. He ought to know the deadly danger he was in.

But didn't he already know? Briefly she hesitated. He knew the attack had been vicious but he couldn't know that it had been, not a robbery but an attempt to take his life.

She had stopped. She now stood there uncertainly, less than a hundred yards from the stage depot. She could go back. She could run home and nothing would happen to her. Nothing was likely to happen to the marshal either.

But she knew it was her fear influencing her thoughts and the realization angered her. Fear wasn't going to dictate her sense of what was right and what was wrong. Determinedly she went on, hurrying so as to cover the last hundred yards before anyone could stop her.

They must have been watching her. They must have watched her almost all the way from her front gate. As she neared the stage depot, they stepped out from the shadows beside it.

Seward Littlejohn, the mortician, said, "Evening, Mrs. Easterday. What are you doing out so late at night?"

She opened her mouth to give the excuse she had rehearsed. She closed it without saying anything.

For several moments she faced the four men. She was

afraid, but in the dark, doubted if they could tell. Finally, she attempted to go on, saying, "Excuse me," and pushing between two of them.

Littlejohn said, "Whoa now. Wait a minute." A hand caught her arm, the fingers biting in as she tried to pull away.

She had, by now, recognized the other three. They were James Dalton, Frank Lane, and Isodoro Chavez. She said coldly, "Let me go."

Littlejohn said, "Nobody's keeping you. It's just that the streets likely ain't safe for a woman this time of night. We'll take you where you're going, Mrs. Easterday."

"That will not be necessary." She couldn't see how she was going to reach Marshal Cragg. Not with these four men escorting her or even watching her. "I am afraid I forgot to blow out the lamp at the restaurant. I was going back to check."

Littlejohn said, "Looks dark to me. What was you really coming down here for, Mrs. Easterday? Couldn't have been you was trying to see that United States Marshal, could it?"

"Why would I want to see him?"

"Why would you want to let him walk you home a while ago? What'd you tell him, and why do you want to see him now?"

"I told you, I want to check the lamp in the restaurant."

"Then let's go do it, and then you can go home." Another hand took her other arm and she found herself being escorted down the street. When they reached the restaurant, Littlejohn said, "Open up, Mrs. Easterday. Let's find out if you left a lamp burning in there."

Numbly she produced her keys and numbly unlocked the door. Littlejohn went in and walked back into the kitchen. When he reappeared, he said, "No lamps burning.

And the fire is out. You can go on home, Mrs. Easterday. Everything's all right down here."

She felt like a mouse, being played with by a cat. There was a mocking tone in Littlejohn's voice that nevertheless also managed to be menacing. She locked the restaurant door. Again she felt both her arms taken and felt herself being escorted firmly if not forcibly along the street, now in the direction of her home. She was not going to be able to warn Marshal Cragg. And she knew that these men were not here for the night air. They meant the marshal harm and if he wasn't warned he might be dead by the time the sun came up.

But she didn't see what she could do. They came abreast the stage depot, two men holding her and gently propelling her along the street, two more bringing up the rear.

Suddenly it made her furious. Never before in her life had she been treated so. Always she had been free to come and go, to do as she pleased without pressure from anyone. Now she was suddenly being treated like a child. She was being prevented from going where she wished to go, doing what she wished to do. She pulled back at the door of the stage depot. She said icily, "Please let me go."

Littlejohn, apparently the spokesman for the group, said, "Now ma'am, it's too late to go calling on folks. Besides, what are the other ladies going to say when they find out you been making late visits to the marshal's room?"

There was still that tolerant mockery in his voice, still that other quality as well, that dangerous, threatening quality. Suddenly she wasn't even sure she would reach home safely.

She tried to pull forcibly away. She managed to pull away from the man on her right but Littlejohn's fingers bit into her arm so hard they hurt. She kicked him in the shins as hard as she could, and heard his stifled cry of surprise and pain. Then she was free, and she darted toward the door of the stage depot.

Her long skirts tripped her and she sprawled helplessly, half in the doorway, half on the walk. She tried to get up, but it was too late. Hands seized her. Littlejohn's voice said angrily, "Get her out of the light! Hurry up, damn it, before somebody sees!"

A hand, a dirty hand, clamped itself over her mouth. She felt herself being dragged away . . .

She knew suddenly, how deadly dangerous this had become. If she didn't get away . . .

She opened her mouth and sank her teeth into the hand that had been clamped over it. She heard the man howl with pain. Desperate, she uttered a single, piercing scream.

All the urgency of her terror, of her certainty that they meant to murder her was in her scream. Then the hand was clamped over her mouth again. She was dragged toward the dark passageway between the stage depot and the building next to it.

Fiercely she struggled, kicking, clawing at their faces. Once more she bit the hand and managed to get out a muffled cry before it was clamped over her mouth again. Littlejohn snarled savagely, "Damn it, drag her out of sight! Her screechin' will raise the whole damn town!"

She could no longer see the lights coming from the saloon across the street. She heard a tin can, kicked by one of her captors, rattle against the wall of the stage depot. She continued to fight, but she knew she was losing, because they had given up dragging her and now were bodily carrying her.

The man in the lead stumbled over something and fell. For an instant, he released her feet.

Twisting her body, she kicked out furiously. Her feet connected with the legs of the other man who had been carrying her and he cursed her angrily. He dropped her and this freed her mouth from the muffling hand. She screamed again.

Distantly she heard pounding footsteps on the boardwalk that ran along this side of Main. She heard a door slam and heard a shot . . .

The four men who had taken her hesitated. A figure loomed up at the end of the passageway. Littlejohn growled, "Let her go! Let's get out of here!"

They were gone, suddenly, their footsteps fading. Something crashed in the alley as one of them fell over it. The figure that had come into the passageway shouted, "What's going on! Sing out, damn it, or I'll shoot!"

Clara Easterday said, "Don't do that, Mr. Cragg. Everything is all right now. They've gone."

Another figure loomed in the entrance to the passageway behind Cragg. The sheriff's voice called, "Cragg? Is that you? What's going on?"

Cragg had reached her and now she saw that all he wore was pants and underwear. Even his feet were bare. She whispered, "I want to talk to you."

Cragg called, "Everything's all right now, Sheriff."

Horsley reached them. "What happened?"

"Some men tried to drag Mrs. Easterday away from the front of the stage depot."

"Why would anybody do a thing like that?"

Cragg didn't reply. He pushed Horsley out of the way and, with a hand on her arm, escorted her back out to the street.

CHAPTER 13

Horsley came along behind, protesting angrily. In front of the stage depot Cragg said: "You seem to have trouble keeping the peace here, Sheriff. You'll have to excuse me if I give you a hand." To Clara he said: "Please come in, Mrs. Easterday. I'll get the rest of my clothes on and then we'll talk. I have a general idea what the people here are trying to hide but maybe it's time I had the particulars."

Clara Easterday knew she could not be in more danger for having told him the town's secret than she had been in when the town thought she was going to tell. He followed her into the stage depot. Kubec was not in the lobby. He led her to the stairs and they climbed it together. He said, "I was about to go to bed. Would you like to wait in the hall? I won't be a minute."

He went into his room, leaving the door ajar. He put on his shirt and pulled on his boots. Then he went to the door and invited her in. He gestured toward the room's single chair. He sat down on the bed himself. Then he waited for her to compose herself and begin.

Horsley watched the pair go into the stage depot. Fury seethed in him, directed almost equally against Cragg for his high-handed statement of a few moments before and the townsmen for their stupidity in attacking Clara Easterday. What the hell had they thought they were going to do with her, he wondered angrily. Did Carberry think she ought to be killed too, along with Cragg and McBee?

He hesitated several moments, trying to decide what he should do. It was certain, now, that Clara Easterday would tell the marshal everything. What Carberry and the others had so desperately wanted to keep secret would now be told because of their own stupidity.

With Cragg knowing everything, including names, the situation would be changed. Carberry could no longer be persuaded to let Cragg leave Broken Butte. He would insist on eliminating Cragg, and McBee, and maybe Clara Easterday as well. Horsley himself would have to get off the fence, however much he disliked doing so. He would have to take sides. He either had to help Carberry and the other members of the mob murder two and possibly three people or he had to put his own life and his career on the line by taking sides with Cragg.

He whirled and for the second time tonight, stalked angrily up the street toward Carberry's house. The front windows were dark but he knew Carberry was still up. He went around to the back, and found light coming from the kitchen windows. He didn't knock, but banged open the door and stepped into the kitchen unannounced.

Four men were there besides Carberry. All had participated in the lynching five months ago. They were Seward Littlejohn, James Dalton, Frank Lane, and Isodoro Chavez. Horsley stood just inside the open door. He could feel his anger growing as he glared at them. Finally he said viciously, "You stupid sons of bitches!"

Carberry blustered, "What's the big idea of barging in here like this? This is a private home!"

Horsley glared at him. "Do you know what these dumb bastards just did? They grabbed Clara Easterday and tried to drag her back into the alley." He switched his glance to the sheepish four. "Just what the hell were you planning to do with her?"

Littlejohn grumbled, "We just thought we could scare her a little bit so she wouldn't tell that marshal anything." Littlejohn was fifty and getting fat. His hair was thinning and he didn't look like a man who would ever be involved in anything violent.

Horsley said savagely, "Well, she didn't scare. She's up in Cragg's room right now telling him everything she knows, including all your names."

The four men looked at Carberry, as if expecting him to make whatever decision needed to be made. Carberry said, "Then it's more important than ever that we get rid of him."

"And how many more?" asked the sheriff bitterly. "McBee, for one, because he knows the marshal got off the stage and stayed in Broken Butte. And Clara Easterday, because she'll know you murdered him. And me, too, because I might be dangerous to you. And then what do you do, start getting rid of each other?"

The prospect was a sobering one for the four, but Carberry must have faced it already in his mind. He said stubbornly, "I'm not going to Yuma no matter what I have to do."

Horsley said, "The trial judge might not send you to Yuma. You might get off with a short jail term. Or even probation. Stranger things have happened."

Carberry's face did not relax its stubborn mold. "It's a chance I'm not going to take. Judge Peckenpaugh would sure as hell disqualify himself because he lives right here and knows us all. They'd bring in an outside judge. No sir. I'm not going to take the chance."

Horsley nodded. He hadn't expected anything else. Sourly he said, "Somebody has to actually pull the trigger. Who's going to do it for you? You're not going to do it yourself, are you?"

Carberry's face was getting redder all the time. He glanced quickly at his four co-conspirators, then at Horsley again. He said, "Get out of here. I don't have anything more to say to you."

Horsley said, "I could arrest you. I could lock you up in jail, at least until the marshal leaves." For a moment he seriously considered it.

But if he had meant to do that he should have done it without issuing a warning first. Carberry nodded at the other men and two of them drew their guns. Carberry said, "Be sensible, Horsley. Go on back down to the jail and shut your eyes and ears."

Horsley nodded reluctantly. He hadn't yet given up entirely but he wasn't making any headway here. He turned, went out the door and pulled it closed behind him. A little chill ran along his spine and his scalp tingled strangely. He admitted that he was afraid. The five men behind him, and possibly the other five, weren't the same men they had been five months ago. They were killers now, because killing is like lying in that one leads to another and to another and another after that. If he had any sense at all, he'd get out of town. Tonight.

Almost imperceptibly he shook his head. What he'd considered good sense was to blame for the fix he now was in. Without his so-called "good sense," the lynching couldn't have occurred because he'd have held his two prisoners whatever the cost had been.

No. This time he'd try to do what he knew was right.

Sitting in the only chair in Gus Cragg's room, Clara Easterday said, "I don't know where to begin."

He said, "Take your time. How long ago did it happen?"

"About five months."

"How many were lynched? More than one?"

"Two."

"Who were they, do you know?"

"I don't think anybody ever knew their names or even took the trouble to ask."

"What were they supposed to have done?"

"Mr. Carberry thought they had killed his daughter. She was Nan's age."

"Who really did kill her?"

"A clerk who worked in Mr. Carberry's store. He had been seeing Eloise." She looked perplexed. "Isn't it terrible how little parents sometimes know about their own children? Eloise had been carrying on with him for months, apparently. She lied to her father that night about where she was going to be—told him she was spending the night with Nan. She and this man took a buggy out on the prairie. Nobody really knows what happened, but I think Eloise tried to make him go away with her by threatening to tell her father and his wife what was going on. He knew Mr. Carberry well enough to know that one would be as bad as the other. No matter what, Mr. Carberry would discharge him and run him out of town, if not worse. His wife would leave him. So he killed her."

"How?"

Clara Easterday was pale. "He must have beaten her to death. Then he ripped off her clothes and scattered them around to make it look as if she had been raped."

Cragg said, "I can see how Carberry would have been almost out of his mind."

"You're not excusing him?"

"No." He studied her for several moments. The more he saw of her and the more he talked with her, the more he liked her. He wondered briefly if Clara Easterday had anything to do with his determination to stay here until he had ferreted out the truth. Probably she did. This wasn't his territory. What he would normally have done was leave and make a report and let the man whose territory it was come here and uncover the truth for himself. But he.knew that he would not and admitted that Clara was the main reason he would not. The other was the fact that they'd tried to beat him to death a while ago with a singletree.

She said, "These two drifters had been in Mr. Carberry's store that afternoon. He decided it must have been them. He got the sheriff and they went after the men. They caught them and brought them back to jail."

"You say it as if it was easy—catching them."

"I guess it was. They were camped just a little ways from town."

"And nobody thought that strange? I'd think if men had murdered a girl they'd put a lot of distance between themselves and the place where it was done."

"Mr. Carberry said it was because they didn't think her body would be found so soon."

"And the sheriff didn't question that?"

"I don't suppose he thought there was any reason why he should. I think he only intended to placate Mr. Carberry by putting the men in jail. I think he meant to go out when it got light and look over the place where Eloise was found. And that's what he did do—the next morning—except that by then it was too late."

Cragg nodded. He knew the rest of the story without asking her. Carberry, half out of his mind with grief and fury, had incited a mob to violence. They had gone to the jail after the two men. The sheriff had been faced with the unpalatable choice of either firing directly into a crowd of his fellow townsmen and friends, or letting them take two men, who might be innocent but who might also be guilty,

out to hang. He had chosen the latter course and next morning had discovered how wrong everyone had been. He
asked, "Did they bring the real killer to trial?"

She nodded. "He was convicted and sent down to Yuma
and hanged."

He grinned ruefully. "And I had to pick this town to lay
over in for a couple of days."

She didn't reply to that. He said, "I'll take you home."

"I'll be all right now. They'll know I told you and they
won't bother me any more."

"I wouldn't be too sure of that." He got up and reached
for his hat. She did not protest further, but went out the
door. Cragg blew out the lamp and followed her.

The lobby was still deserted. So was the street when
they stepped into it. The saloon was closed, but a single
lamp burned in its interior. Cragg started walking toward
Clara's house and she took his arm and kept pace with him.

It had been a long time since the mere touch of a
woman's hand on his arm had stirred him so. He said, "You
won't be able to stay here in Broken Butte."

"I know."

"Had you thought of that when you decided to tell me
what had happened here?"

"Yes. Maybe I didn't want to stay here any longer anyway. What happened five months ago has changed the
town. The people are not the same. Before the lynching I
wouldn't have believed it possible that the respectable men
who live here would try to kill you or that they would drag
me off the street and threaten me."

"Where will you go?"

"I haven't thought that far ahead."

Without seeming to, he kept an eye on the shadows,
prodded by an uneasiness that he knew was more instinct
than anything. They reached her house without incident.

He walked with her around the house to the kitchen door, which was ajar. A lamp, which had been turned down, was on the table.

Clara, her eyes suddenly frightened, left him and hurried through the kitchen and into the darkened part of the house beyond. He heard no scream, but he somehow knew that Nan was gone. When Clara returned, her face was very pale. "She's gone."

He said, "I'll find her, but you've got to do what I tell you to."

She nodded wordlessly, her eyes fixed on his face. He said, "Lock your door. Don't let anybody in, even if they use Nan's name to try and get you to open up. Have you got a gun?"

"Yes."

"Get it and load it. Shoot anybody that breaks in. Can you do that?"

She nodded again and he believed that she really could. He crossed the room and put his hands on her shoulders. He kissed her on the forehead. "I'll come back for you as soon as I find the sheriff," he said.

She nodded. He crossed to the door and went out. He waited until he heard the bolt. Then he headed for the jail.

CHAPTER 14

Nan Easterday was in bed when they entered the house and came upstairs. At first she thought the sound of the door opening was her mother coming in. Hearing several people crossing the kitchen floor still did not alarm her. Only when the men actually came into her bedroom did she feel a touch of fear.

She knew every one of them. Their leader was Mr. Littlejohn. His face was shiny with sweat. He said, "There's nothing to be afraid of, Nan. We just want you to come with us."

"Why?"

"It's your mother. She's been hurt."

Nan immediately jumped out of bed. The men retired discreetly to give her an opportunity to dress in private. It only took her two or three minutes. Then she came running from her bedroom. "Where is she? What's happened to her?"

Littlejohn said, "You'll see. Come on."

"Is she . . ."

Littlejohn said, "Come on. Hurry."

They went out, with Nan accompanying them willingly. If she thought it strange that they went up the alley instead of the street, she did not comment. They reached Eric Carberry's house, but they did not go in. Instead, the men took her into Carberry's stable at the rear of the house. One of them lighted a lantern.

Nan looked around. Her mother wasn't here. She said, "Mother . . . where is she?"

Littlejohn said, "She isn't here. Nothing has happened to her. Now you just keep still and everything will be all right."

"I want to go home."

"You can't. We're going to keep you here for a little while. Until your mother and that federal marshal decide to be reasonable."

Nan broke for the door but one of the men caught and held her. She opened her mouth to scream for help, but a hand was clapped over it.

Isodoro Chavez said, "Don't hurt her."

Littlejohn said, "Shut up."

Chavez said, "I mean it. Don't hurt her."

Littlejohn said sarcastically, "Maybe you'd rather go to Yuma for a few years."

Chavez said stubbornly, "Maybe I would. Maybe even Yuma is better than the things we're doing. First it was her mother and now her. Who's it going to be next?"

Littlejohn said, "Maybe the rest of you don't know what Yuma is like. I do. I was down there several years ago and I got a look at the prison. It's like hell on earth. Every day is like a year. And if you break out, they pay the Indians to get you back. Only they don't bring back all of you. Just your leg, with the bloody marks of the iron on the ankle."

Chavez asked, "How's hurting this girl going to keep us out of Yuma?"

"Because that marshal ain't going to push the thing if he knows she'll be killed if he does."

"We can't keep her forever."

"We won't have to. Soon's we get our hands on him . . ."

"You mean we're going to kill him too?"

"That's what Carberry says."

"And what about Horsley? Are we going to kill him too?"

Littlejohn said, "How the hell do I know? Ask Carberry. I figure he's trying to keep himself out of Yuma and the more we help him the more we help ourselves."

Chavez said, "All the same, we ain't going to hurt this girl." He crossed to Nan, being held by one of the other men. He said, "Don't you worry none. We ain't going to keep you very long. You just keep still and don't try to run away and I'll see that you don't get hurt."

She made no sound. One of the men said, "Where's Carberry?"

Littlejohn said, "Up at the house. I'll get him. Maybe he'll tell us what we ought to do."

Chavez said, "Sure. Like he told us what to do the night we hanged those two strangers for something they hadn't done."

Littlejohn said, "You better watch your tongue. If Carberry was to hear . . ."

"Then you'd kill me too? Maybe we ought to just kill everybody in town. Then we'd be sure nobody would tell. After that we'd have to start killing each other off."

Frank Lane said, "Shut up, Chavez. It ain't near as bad as you make it sound. All we're trying to do is stay out of Yuma. It ain't going to help those two we hanged if all of us go to prison, is it?"

"The judge might not send us there. It was a mistake. The town was all worked up over Eloise Carberry being killed and we made a mistake."

Littlejohn said, "We don't intend to take the chance."

Lane said, "Go get Carberry. Standing here arguing won't solve anything."

Littlejohn went out the stable door. The man holding Nan said, "If I take my hand away will you keep still?"

She nodded and the man took his hand away. She asked in a scared, small voice, "What are you going to do with me?"

"Just keep you for a couple of hours. Until the marshal decides not to put up a fight."

Her voice was still small but it was determined too, "You're all just making things worse. It was awful enough when you hanged those men but that *was* a mistake. What you're doing now isn't a mistake, it's a crime."

Nobody said anything. Littlejohn returned, followed by Carberry. Carberry said, "Don't be frightened, Nan. You're not going to be hurt."

She said, "It's no wonder Eloise didn't like you much."

He stared furiously at her. "That's a lie!"

"No it isn't. She told me about you. She was just trying to hurt you, going with the clerk that worked in your store."

Carberry slapped her on the side of the face. Chavez said, "Stop it! What's the use of that?"

Littlejohn asked, "What should we do with her?"

Carberry replied angrily, "You should have left her alone, but it's too late now. Get her out of town. This is the first place the marshal and Horsley will look for her."

"Where should we take her?"

"That shack of mine out in the creek bottom. Take some food and water and stay with her until you hear from me. Maybe if all four of you are out of town you won't make any more stupid mistakes. I'll decide what to do and come let you know."

"You told us to jump Cragg."

"But I didn't tell you to drag Clara into the alley and I didn't tell you to kidnap Nan."

Sullenly the four men left, taking Nan along with them. She had promised not to scream but apparently they didn't believe her because they had put a gag over her mouth.

Carberry watched them go, scowling angrily. Then he blew out the flickering lantern and returned to the house.

Carberry had not been inside for more than five or ten minutes before the sheriff and Cragg arrived. With them was Clara Easterday. Horsley pushed into the kitchen and Clara followed. Cragg brought up the rear. Horsley asked angrily, "Where is she?"

"Where is who?"

"Nan. Somebody took her from her home and I figure you know who."

"Well I don't. Why would anybody take Nan Easterday?"

"To put pressure on the marshal and me."

Carberry shrugged. Horsley said, "I'm going to look in the stable." He left and came back a few moments later. "They were out there all right. The lantern's still warm."

"It's no crime for a man to go to his own stable at night."

Horsley said, "You're only making it worse for yourself. Lynching those two men was bad enough. Trying to kill a U. S. Marshal is only adding to your trouble and kidnapping a little girl is practically begging for a cell at Yuma. You must be out of your mind!"

"Nobody's out of his mind and I didn't kidnap Nan. But if I had, do you know what advice I'd give to you?"

Suspiciously Horsley asked, "What?"

"I'd advise you to go home. Go to bed. I'd tell you that Nan's safety would be best assured if you did that."

Clara Easterday had not, until now, said anything. "Mr. Carberry, Nan was Eloise's friend."

"Some friend! Lying for Eloise while she was out on the prairie with . . ." He stopped, fists clenched, trying to control himself.

Clara said, "Nan didn't know anything about that."

Carberry opened his mouth, thought better of what he had intended to say, and closed it again. He gained control of himself with difficulty. He said with enforced calm, "If that's all, I'd appreciate your leaving so that I can go to bed."

Clara looked at Horsley, then at Cragg. Horsley said, "Come on, Clara. Nan will be all right. They wouldn't dare do anything to her."

She went out doubtfully into the night. Cragg followed her. Horsley waited long enough to say, "You've gone too far, Carberry. You'd better backtrack while there's time. Send Nan home."

"I don't know what you're talking about."

Horsley stalked out the door. Carberry slammed it behind him and shot the bolt. Clara Easterday asked, "What do we do now? Isn't there someway he can be made to tell? I'm scared."

Horsley said, "They won't hurt Nan."

"What do they want us to do?"

"We'll get the word soon enough." He turned his head and looked back at Carberry's house. Cragg said, "He won't go to bed. Just as soon as he thinks it's safe, he'll go wherever they're holding her."

"Then can't we just stay here and follow him when he goes?"

Horsley said softly, "Somebody's probably watching us. The thing for us to do is to go home like Carberry said. Pretend to go to bed, give whoever's watching us time to leave, and then slip out again."

Clara said in a frightened voice, "All right."

Horsley said to Cragg, "You see her home. Then go back to the stage depot. Go up and light your lamp, then blow it out. Come out the back door. Meet me down at the jail."

"All right."

Horsley disappeared into the darkness. Cragg took Clara's arm. In silence they walked out to the street and along it to Clara's house. She unlocked the door and went inside. He cautioned, "Don't blow out the lamp right away. I'll be back as soon as I can."

"Be careful. It's you they really want."

"Sure." He waited until she had lighted a lamp and bolted the door. Then he headed for the stage depot, walking in the middle of the street to make another attack more difficult and dangerous for them.

He reached the stage depot without incident. He went in, climbed the stairs and went into his room. He stepped in quickly, his gun in his hand, but there was no one waiting for him.

He lighted the lamp. He went to the window and pulled the shade. He sat down on the edge of the bed and waited several minutes. Then he blew out the lamp and raised the shade.

He could see no one in the street but that didn't mean no one was there. He went quietly to the door, opened it and stepped out into the hall.

He knew there was a back stairway because he had seen it earlier. He walked along the hall as quietly as he could but the floor squeaked thunderously.

He reached the stairs and went quickly down. He opened the outside door and stepped out into the night.

He could see the outhouses and the pump where the stage passengers had been told to wash. He stood there in the shadows for a long time, looking for movement, listening.

He had been a lawman all his life so this kind of thing

was not exactly new to him. But it still made his heart beat faster, still put a slight tremor into his knees.

Walking as silently as a cat, he headed for the alley. Reaching it, he turned toward the jail.

CHAPTER 15

Eric Carberry stared angrily at the door for a long time after it closed behind Clara Easterday, Horsley, and Cragg, the U. S. Marshal. Attacking Cragg had been a serious mistake. It might not have been so bad if the attackers hadn't bungled it, if they had killed Cragg the way they had intended. But they *had* bungled it.

Then they had tried dragging Clara into the alley to frighten her into cutting off all contact with Marshal Cragg. That had gone wrong too. Their latest folly had been the kidnapping of Nan Easterday.

He paced nervously back and forth, a big man with a homely, usually pleasant face whom no one would ever suspect of a crime of violence. If all four, Cragg, Horsley, Clara, and Nan could be gotten rid of together, in a way that seemed accidental, there would be no need for getting rid of McBee. Maybe the killing could end. Maybe the town could get back to normal again and maybe eventually the lynching and the subsequent killings would be forgotten or at least put out of people's minds.

An accidental death for four people. There was only one believable way it could be done. By fire. And the house in which they perished had to be Clara Easterday's.

Now the trick was going to be getting them all together in one place. They had to be overcome, knocked unconscious and placed in Clara's house which could then be set afire. With their deaths the nightmare begun by Eloise's murder could end at last.

But he was going to need the help of every one of the nine men who had participated in the lynching of the two drifters five months ago and four were with Nan out at the shack in the river bottom three miles from town. He'd have to send someone to bring them back.

Only when they all were back here in town could they move against Horsley, Cragg, and Clara Easterday. He didn't dare risk trying to take Cragg and Horsley with an insufficient force.

He blew out the lamp. He listened. He didn't know whether his wife was still asleep or not. All the shouting and accusations down here a while ago had probably awakened her. If so, she would know he had left but she would have no way of knowing why. Even if she did find out later what he and the others had done, she wouldn't dare say anything.

He heard no sound upstairs. Silently, he went out the back door. He stood for several moments, listening. Then, reasonably sure he was not being watched, he headed for Clara Easterday's. He found it dark. Going by the stage depot he satisfied himself that the marshal's room was also dark. So was the jail. Satisfied that the three had taken his advice he headed for Tom Bowen's house.

Bowen was apparently asleep. Carberry pounded on the back door until he heard Bowen's sleepy, protesting voice from the upstairs window. Bowen stuck out his head. "What do you want?"

"Get dressed and come down. Right away."

Recognizing Carberry's voice, Bowen didn't protest any more. Carberry waited and after a few moments he saw a lamp's light descending the stairs, growing stronger as it approached the door. Bowen opened it and Carberry said, "Blow out that lamp."

Bowen obeyed. Carberry said, "I want you to go get Howie Depew. Tell him to wake Fender and you go wake Roth Anderson. Have one of them stop by the stage depot and get Kubec. Then all of you meet at my house. In the stable, so my wife won't be disturbed."

"What's up?"

"Never mind now. But if you want to stay out of Yuma, you'd better do exactly what I say."

That frightened Bowen. His voice was scared as he said, "All right. We'll be there in ten minutes at the outside."

Carberry left. He hurried back to his own house. He went into the stable and lighted the lantern.

His two horses moved around restlessly in their stalls. Carberry forced himself to sit down on an overturned, empty nail keg. He'd be glad when this was all over with.

He'd made his first mistake when he'd assumed the federal marshal was here to investigate the lynchings. Since then, mistake had piled upon mistake, not all of them made by any one person but all brought about by fear on the part of the men who had helped hang the two strangers five months ago. They would all have to see to it that no more mistakes were made. Tonight had to end it, with the fire at Clara Easterday's.

Someone was sure to come, eventually, to look into the marshal's death. But if everybody kept calm and didn't panic, the investigator would go away satisfied that nothing was amiss.

Nervously he waited. Bowen was the first to arrive. He came into the stable, sweating and out of breath, and said, "They're on their way."

"All right. Sit down."

Bowen looked around for a place to sit. Finally he sat

on the edge of the grain bin. He didn't press Carberry to tell him what was going on.

Depew came next, accompanied by Bill Fender. They came in and Carberry said, "Find a place to sit down. I'll tell you all about it when the others get here."

Anderson and Kubec arrived last, having apparently met each other coming up the street. They were all here now. Carberry said, "We're all going to Yuma if we don't work together. That federal marshal knows what happened here five months ago. He even knows our names."

"What are we going to do?" asked Depew.

"We've got to get rid of him. And Horsley. And Clara Easterday and her daughter Nan."

He hit them with it all at once. It would shock them and some of them would balk but he knew how scared all of them were of the thought of being sent to Yuma.

Anderson asked in a thin, scared voice, "Why Clara and Nan?"

"Clara is the one who told the marshal all the details. If she'd tell him she'll tell someone else. And if she goes, Nan has also got to go."

Kubec, sweating so much that his whole face was shiny with it, said, "Jesus!"

Bowen said, "No. I ain't going to have any part of killing those two."

Carberry looked at him. "Maybe you'd rather go to Yuma for what we did five months ago."

"No. But killing a woman and a girl is something I ain't going to have any part of."

Carberry stared at him. He was aware that if Bowen got away with defying him it would encourage others to do the same. He was also aware that he had to have one hundred per cent co-operation from all the men who had been involved. He said, "You got to fish or cut bait, Bowen.

You're either with the rest of us or you're against us. And I'm going to tell you the goddam truth—we can't afford anybody against us. You understand what I mean?"

Bowen understood all right. He looked at Carberry, then around at the other men in turn. Carberry had nipped Bowen's rebellion in the bud. The faces of the other four were hard and hostile and Bowen finally nodded reluctantly. "All right, all right. I ain't against you. I'm in it as deep as anybody."

Carberry nodded. "All right then. Let's not have any more foolish talk. Fender, take one of my horses and go out to that shack of mine in the river bottom. They're holding Nan out there. As soon as you all get back, we'll pick up the sheriff and the marshal and take them up to the Easterday house."

Fender saddled and bridled one of the two horses fidgeting in their stalls. He led him out the door, mounted and rode away at a walk. Carberry said, "It'll be an hour, probably, before they get back. Does anybody want a drink?"

A couple of the men said they did. Carberry went to the house, slipped in quietly and got a bottle of whiskey. He took it out to the stable, uncorked it and handed it to the nearest man. The bottle made the rounds and made the rounds again. Carberry didn't try to slow them down. They'd be easier to manage if they'd had a few drinks than if they were cold sober.

He didn't anticipate any trouble with Horsley. The sheriff would hesitate about shooting into them just as he had five months ago. He'd hesitate until it was too late.

But that United States Marshal, Cragg, was something else. Carberry's chest suddenly felt cold. He looked down at his knees and saw they were trembling. He crossed his legs to conceal it from the other men.

He was afraid of Cragg but he had to overcome it, because Cragg had to be gotten rid of tonight. Otherwise, he might spend the rest of his life in that hellhole at Yuma where more men perished than ever were released.

CHAPTER 16

Cragg reached the sheriff's office from the alley. He rounded it silently and, peering around the corner, saw Horsley standing in the shadows waiting for him. He said softly, "Let's go."

Horsley joined him. Cragg led the way back to the alley, and turned uptown. He crossed Willow but stopped for a couple of minutes short of the rear door of the stage depot. He saw nothing and heard nothing and so went on. So far Horsley hadn't said anything.

Cragg crossed Maple quickly and silently, then cut through a yard heading for Clara Easterday's. A dog, startled, began to bark frantically. Cragg broke into a trot crossing Main and ran up Clara's path. The door was open and the two men went inside. Cragg muttered, "Damn that dog!"

Clara said, "He'll quiet down in a minute or so. We can slip out the back."

The two men followed her through the dark house to the back door. They stepped out into the back yard and Clara closed the door. Cragg said, "Sheriff, lead the way to Carberry's house."

Horsley headed up the alley. Gravel grated beneath his feet. Cragg kept hoping no more dogs would hear them and begin to bark. They reached the unnamed alley that marked the town's western boundary. It was dusty and overgrown with weeds.

Where the alleyway crossed Main, Horsley stopped. He stared across at Carberry's house. "He may already have left but we'll soon find out."

He hurried across Main. On the far side the stable was visible. Light was coming from a few cracks in the building walls. Horsley whispered, "He's still there. Or someone is."

A square of light became visible as the stable door opened. Two men slipped in and closed it again. Horsley said, "I can't be sure, but those two looked like Kubec and Anderson."

Cragg whispered to Clara, "I think we're in time. I don't think anybody has gone after the ones who kidnapped Nan."

It was warm, almost hot, but Clara Easterday was shivering. Cragg laid a hand on her shoulder. "Don't worry. It will be all right."

She did not reply, but her shivering lessened. They waited. They could hear the soft murmur of voices coming from inside the stable. After a while the door opened again and a man came out, leading a horse. Horsley said, "Damn. We've got to get horses and get them fast."

Cragg said, "You follow on foot long enough to see which way he goes. Mrs. Easterday, have you got a buggy or buckboard or something?"

"I have a buckboard."

"Let's get it." He trotted back toward her house. Lifting her skirts, she came hurrying along behind.

Horsley followed the rider, who proceeded at a walk down the middle of Main where the dust was deep and would muffle the sound of his horse's hoofs. Cragg and Clara reached the stable at the rear of her house. Cragg lighted a lantern and by its light swiftly harnessed Clara's team. He backed them to the buckboard and hitched up.

Clara was already on the seat. He blew out the lantern, climbed up beside her and drove out of the stable. He said, "If that rider was going east on Main, where do you think he might be headed?"

She was silent a moment, thinking. Finally she said, "Mr. Carberry owns some land along the creek bottom. There's a little shack on it."

"Then that must be where they are."

"How can we follow a horseman with a buckboard? He'll hear us, won't he?"

"Not if we stay back far enough."

He reached the bridge at the foot of Main. It was about seventy-five feet long, spanning the creek which was only a trickle in the middle of a wide stream bed. To one side was a detour, probably for freight wagons too heavy for the bridge. Cragg took it to avoid making noise crossing the bridge. Horsley was waiting for them on the other side. He climbed up, crowding Clara close against Cragg as he sat down. He said, "He's headed toward Carberry's shack. There's a road that turns left about a quarter mile farther on."

Cragg kept the horses at a walk. When he reached the turnoff he took it.

Once, Clara whispered, "What are they going to do with her?"

Cragg said quickly, "They won't hurt her, if that's what you're worried about. She's no good to them except as a hostage to make us do what they want us to."

"And what is that?"

Cragg didn't know what was the best way to answer her. He knew what Carberry wanted. The attack on him earlier had told him that. Carberry wanted him dead. He probably also wanted Horsley dead and, if he suspected

Clara or her daughter would talk, likely intended to also murder them.

Clara said, "I want to know."

Cragg said, "All right. They want me dead. They can't afford to let me leave because they know I'll report what happened here. I don't know what they intend to do about the sheriff or about you and your daughter Nan. I guess that depends on whether they think you will keep still."

Clara said, "By now they know I won't."

"I'm not trying to scare you, but I guess you've answered your own question."

She was silent for a long time. Finally she said, "It's so hard to believe. I've known every one of them for years."

Cragg said, "Men change when they're scared."

They traveled in silence for a long time afterward. Once, Cragg got down and, with a match, examined the horse tracks in the narrow road they were following. When he climbed back up, he said, "We're still following."

"What are we going to do when we get there?"

Cragg didn't know. They'd be outnumbered. He figured the same four who had attacked him had kidnapped Nan Easterday. With the man sent by Carberry to warn them, it would make five. On the other hand, none of the five was used to violence as both Cragg and the sheriff were.

Clara Easterday repeated, "What can we do?"

Horsley answered her, "I'll call on them to surrender themselves and give Nan up."

"What if they refuse?"

"We'll face that possibility when we have to."

Finally, ahead, they saw a faint and flickering light. Cragg slowed slightly. They approached until they were within about three hundred yards. Then Cragg pulled the rig off the road. He got down. "Stay here, Mrs. Easterday."

She asked, "Can't I . . . ?" and stopped. Reluctantly she said, "All right."

Neither Cragg nor Horsley answered her. They moved away on foot, close to the road but not on it. Out of hearing, Cragg asked, "Will she stay put?"

"I think so. She's a good woman, Mr. Cragg."

"I can see that." He was hurrying. He didn't know how long Carberry's messenger had been at the shack, but he must have been five or ten minutes ahead of them. His message had probably been to come back to town, bringing Nan along. The five, and Nan, could be leaving the shack at any time. He wanted to get there before they left.

A hundred feet from the shack, Cragg released a sigh of relief. There were five horses tied in front of the shack. All five men still were here.

Horsley asked, "Now what do we do?"

"Well, we don't want to shoot it out with them. The girl might get hurt. I'd say your best bet would be to call out and tell them to give themselves up. Tell them it will go a lot easier for them if they do."

"They're in pretty deep. Maybe they won't give up."

"If they don't, then we can shoot it out with them."

"I guess you're right." Horsley cleared his throat. He bawled, "Hey! In the cabin! This is Horsley! I know you've got Nan Easterday! Give yourselves up and it'll go a lot easier."

There was utter silence down at the shack. The lamp went out. Cragg and Horsley eased closer, ready to shoot the horses if the men in the shack tried to make a break for it.

A gun flashed from the cabin door. The bullet struck the ground fifty feet from Cragg and Horsley and whined away. Both men waited. Those in the cabin would either give themselves up or they would not but in either case they needed a few minutes to make up their minds.

Finally someone yelled from the cabin. "Sheriff?"

"What?"

"You alone out there?"

Horsley turned his head to look at Cragg. "What should I say?"

"Tell 'em yes, that you're alone."

Horsley yelled, "Sure I'm alone. But that's got nothing to do with it. You men are breaking the law. You're getting in deeper all the time."

The voice yelled back, "Come on in, Sheriff. Without your gun. If you don't, we'll kill this girl."

Horsley yelled, "No you won't. You men aren't murderers. Now give yourselves up and let Nan go."

There was a note of desperation in the voice that shouted back, "You're crazy, Sheriff, if you think we won't kill Nan! What the hell have we got to lose? That marshal's going to send us to Yuma for that lynching five months ago. You get the same sentence for three murders as you do for two!"

Horsley yelled, "Don't be stupid! There's a big difference between lynching two men you think have killed a girl and killing a girl yourselves in cold blood."

The same man yelled impatiently, "Damn it, I ain't going to argue with you all night. Either you come in or we kill her. You got just one minute to make up your mind!"

Cragg asked, "What do you think? Will they do it?"

Horsley said, "I'm damned if I know whether they'll do it or not."

"What will they do to you if you go in and surrender yourself?"

"Nothing right away. They won't kill either Nan or me without getting Carberry's approval."

"Then you'd better go on in. Let them think that you're alone. I'll get you out of it."

Horsley hesitated, but only briefly. Finally he said, "I sure as hell hope you do."

Turning he yelled, "All right. I'm coming in. I'll drop my gun out in the yard."

He walked toward the shack. Cragg heard the door squeak and a few moments later saw the flicker of light as somebody lighted the lamp.

He wasn't sure he had advised Horsley properly but he didn't see what else he could have done. The two of them couldn't have rescued Nan by shooting it out with her kidnappers, and they might have wounded or even killed her by trying. There had been no other choice. At least he was still free and armed.

He backtracked to where he had left Clara and the buckboard. He called to her as he approached to avoid frightening her. She asked immediately, as he climbed to the buckboard seat, "Where is the sheriff?"

"They threatened to kill Nan if he didn't give himself up."

She was silent but he knew how terrified she was. She said, "Now they have two hostages."

"Yes."

"What can we do?"

"I don't know. We'll follow them back to town." He slapped the horses' backs with the reins and drove the rig farther from the road so that there would be no chance of its being seen. He said, "Get close enough to the road so that you can count the horses that go by. I want to be sure they didn't leave anybody behind."

"What are you going to do?"

"Keep the horses quiet. The wind's blowing from the road toward us and they may nicker if they smell the other horses going by." He climbed down from the seat and went to the horses. He put a hand on the nose of each, ready to cover their nostrils if they showed any indication that they smelled the horses going by. Clara moved quietly into the darkness and disappeared.

He heard hoofbeats on the road. They grew louder, then diminished as they went along the road toward town.

Clara Easterday came back. "I counted five horses. The riders on two of them were doubled up."

"All right. Come on." He helped her to the buckboard seat and then climbed up himself. She said, "One of those riding double was Nan. She must be scared to death."

With more conviction than he felt he said, "She'll be all right. Nothing is going to happen to her."

After a thoughtful pause Clara replied, "I don't know what's happening to this town. Five months ago it changed. It scares me now."

It scared Cragg too because he knew how savage a mob of frightened men could be.

CHAPTER 17

The inside of the little shack was steaming hot. Five men were there, and Nan, and Horsley himself. The lamp sent a thin plume of black smoke toward the pole ceiling, which was covered with brush and earth to keep out the rain.

It was also jammed. Only twelve feet by ten, and with a double bunk at one end and a table and benches in the middle, the seven people filled it to overflowing.

All five of the men had guns. Horsley said disgustedly, "You're acting like a bunch of stupid kids. Let Nan go and you all go on home to bed and I'll try to forget what happened tonight."

Seward Littlejohn, who seemed to be their leader, said, "It ain't stupid to try and stay out of Yuma, Sheriff, and that's what we're trying to do."

"And is killing me, and Nan, and her mother and that U. S. Marshal going to keep you out of Yuma?"

"Nobody said anything about killing you," Littlejohn said sullenly.

"No? Then what do *you* think the end of all this is going to be? What do *you* think Carberry has in mind?"

"Maybe trying to reason with you. And with the marshal."

"Fine. Go ahead and reason with me. What do you want from me, a promise that I'll keep still? You've got it. You want a promise that Nan will keep still? Tell them, Nan. Tell them you won't breathe a word."

Nan said fearfully, "I won't. Honest I won't."

Littlejohn said, "That's not enough."

"Then what is enough? Do any of you know?" He looked around at the men. Besides Littlejohn there was Fender, probably the one who had ridden here with Carberry's message and there was Frank Lane, and Jim Dalton and Isodoro Chavez.

Every one of them was a law-abiding man. Or at least every one of them had been until five months ago. Horsley said, "You men ought to be able to see that you're digging yourselves in deeper all the time. First it was a lynching. Then attempted murder of a U. S. Marshal. Now it's kidnapping and before the night's over it's going to be cold-blooded, premeditated murder. For that you can go to Yuma for life."

Chavez said, "He's right. I say we ought to let him go. And Nan. I ain't going to be no part of hurting either one of them."

Littlejohn scowled fiercely at him. He said brutally, "You Mexican son-of-a-bitch, who asked you what you thought? You'll go along with what the rest of us do or you'll end up in the same grave with them."

Chavez's face darkened at the epithet. "Then you do intend to murder them."

"I didn't say that." Littlejohn was watching Horsley closely.

"The hell you didn't." Chavez looked around at the other men. He said, "Frank, you ain't going to stand for murdering four people, are you?"

Lane avoided meeting his glance directly. He mumbled, "We got to stick together in this thing. Hell, even you can see that. I don't like it any more than you, but we got to stick together."

Chavez said disgustedly, "Christ!" He looked at Dalton. Horsley could see that Dalton's expression, while ashamed, was as unyielding as Lane's. Chavez looked at Fender. Fender started to look away, then raised his eyes and stared defiantly at Littlejohn. "He's right. Four more killings are going to make us feel a hell of a sight worse than we do now."

Littlejohn said, "I'd rather feel bad in Broken Butte than to feel good down at Yuma. I don't know about you, but I've heard what that damn place is like. Six men to a cell and the cell no bigger than eight by eight. And the hole. It's down in the ground, maybe eight or ten feet square, and an iron trap door over the top of it. No air, the floor slimy with your own filth, no place to lie down and the smell bad enough to make the guards vomit when they raise the door. The men they put down there either die or go mad. Is that what you want?"

Nan began to cry. She tried to control herself but she couldn't stop either her sobs or the tears that welled from her eyes and rolled down her cheeks. She looked at Horsley and asked between sobs, "Is Mama all right?"

"Sure, honey. She's all right."

Littlejohn asked, "How do you know that? Is she outside?"

"I didn't say she was outside. I said she was all right."

"If you're so sure of that, she must be outside. And that U. S. Marshal with her."

Horsley felt a tightness in his chest. If they thought Cragg and Clara were out there in the darkness, they might try to make them surrender themselves by once more threatening Nan.

Littlejohn went to the door. He opened it and peered into the darkness. Lane said, "Don't stand there in the door. He might shoot you."

"Huh-uh. He knows what would happen to Nan and Horsley if he did." He shut the door and crossed the room to Nan. He seized her and brought her arm up behind her back. He said, "Go ahead. Yell your fool head off."

Nan bit her lip and made no sound. Littlejohn raised the arm nearer to her shoulder blades. She bit down harder on her lip until a drop of blood ran from it and trickled across her chin.

Horsley and Chavez moved toward Littlejohn at the same time. Horsley reached him first. His fist exploded against the side of Littlejohn's head and the man let go of Nan and staggered against the wall. When he whirled toward the sheriff his face was livid, his finger tight on the trigger of his gun. Chavez stepped between him and Horsley. He said, "All right. If you're goin' to shoot, go ahead and shoot."

Littlejohn lowered the gun. He said, "It's stupid to fight among ourselves."

Chavez said, "Then let's quit hurting kids."

"You were in on trying to scare her ma."

Fender said, "For God's sake, quit bickering. Carberry said to bring the girl back to town. I'd suggest that's what we do."

"And what if the marshal *is* out there? He can pick us off one by one."

"Not without risking the lives of Horsley and the girl."

"You think he cares about their lives?"

Chavez said, "Yes. I think he cares. He's a lawman and he's got honor because he is."

Horsley felt his face darkening with shame. He was also a lawman but most of his honor had gotten away from him the night of the lynching five months ago. If he let any of what was left get away he'd have trouble living with himself all the rest of his life.

Littlejohn said, "All right, let's get back to town. Nobody here seems to be able to agree. Maybe Carberry can decide what ought to be done."

Nobody protested. Horsley wondered what Cragg would do. He didn't think the marshal would risk the lives of two hostages trying to take five men. But he wasn't sure. One thing he was sure of, though. If Cragg did attack, he would be the first to die.

Leaving the lamp burning, the men trooped out to their horses. Chavez took Nan's hand and led her to his horse. He lifted her up, then mounted behind her. Littlejohn asked, "Where's your horse, Sheriff?"

Horsley looked around, as if trying to pierce the darkness. "The son-of-a-bitch must've gone back to town. I left him here." Even as he said it, he doubted if he would be believed. A loose horse wouldn't go back to town on his own as long as five other horses were standing tied nearby. But these were townsmen, and perhaps that was why they did not challenge him. Littlejohn said, "All right, you ride with one of us."

"With who?"

Fender said, "You can ride with me."

Littlejohn stayed on the ground until everyone was mounted. Then he went in and blew out the lamp. He closed the door so that cattle wouldn't get in, mounted and led off toward town.

Horsley wondered where Cragg and Clara were. Somewhere in the darkness watching, he supposed.

Calling on the men to surrender had been a mistake. Now he was a prisoner along with Nan, and unable to help Cragg. The only good he might do was to try and keep them from hurting Nan.

The little cavalcade plodded through the darkness toward town. Nan was silent but he knew she must be terrified. He wished he could talk to her alone and tell her that her mother was safe with Cragg.

It was a little more than a couple of miles to town but it seemed like less. The five horses strung out on the road, with little talking back and forth between the men. Once, Horsley asked, "You in favor of what Carberry plans to do?"

Fender said, "Hell no, I'm not. But I'm only one. There's ten of us, remember?"

"Maybe some of the others feel like you do."

"Maybe. But we're all in it together and we're going to do whatever we have to do to stay out of prison."

"You might not get sent to prison. How do you know what a judge or a jury will say?"

"Would *you* take the chance? Even if we only got five years none of us would come out of Yuma alive."

"Commit four murders and you'll hang or go to Yuma for life."

"What's the difference? Life is from the time you go in until the time you die."

"Maybe Yuma isn't that bad."

"And maybe it's worse. You'd just as well save your breath, Sheriff. You're not going to talk me out of anything."

Horsley said, "Bill . . ."

"Shut up. If you'd done right five months ago we wouldn't be in this fix. This is as much your fault as it is ours."

And, Horsley had to admit, what he said was true.

Cragg felt a little better about Nan now that the Sheriff was with her captors. Horsley wouldn't let them do anything to her without putting up a fight. The sheriff might have caused the lynching five months ago by weakness and indecision, but he had stiffened up.

Cragg couldn't find it in himself to condemn the sheriff for his hesitation five months before. It was easy enough to say that he should have done his sworn duty no matter what. But it wasn't ever that simple. The sheriff had known every one of the ten members of the lynch mob. He had known them well, had known their families. He had probably considered some of them close friends. It wouldn't have been easy for him to fire a shotgun point-blank into their ranks. It might not even have been possible.

Clara sat beside him on the seat, straight and erect. He knew how scared she was. Suddenly he put an arm around her shoulders and briefly hugged her close to him. She raised her face to look at him and, in starlight, he caught the shine of tears upon her cheeks.

She asked, her voice shaking, "What are we going to do?"

"Well, I figure Carberry is the one that's pushing everything. Without him, maybe the others would come apart. We'll go back to town. Maybe I can get Carberry."

"And if you can't?"

He said, "Don't you give up yet."

"They made the sheriff give himself up by threatening Nan. What if they try the same threat on you?"

He didn't know what to say. If he believed their threat, he supposed he would give himself up the way the sheriff had. But he didn't think they'd harm Nan or the sheriff as long as he was free. They wouldn't dare because his testimony could put them in Yuma Penitentiary, or get them executed if they harmed the pair.

He said, "Nan's only chance, and yours, and the sheriff's, depends on keeping them scared of me. They won't hurt her, no matter how they threaten, as long as they don't have me."

His answer didn't satisfy her. He could tell that it did

not. But then nothing he could have said would have satisfied her, any more than any alternative he could think of would wholly satisfy him.

Only one thing he knew for sure. When the mob had all four of them then hope would finally be gone.

CHAPTER 18

Cragg did not take the buckboard all the way into town. He halted it on the outskirts, snapped the tether weight to the bridle of one of the horses and then helped Clara Easterday to the ground. "We'll leave the buckboard here. Do you know someplace you can hide while I see if I can get to Carberry?"

"I want to go with you."

"I know you do, but it's too risky. I can get around faster and more quietly if you aren't along."

She said, "I can stay here."

"All right. I'll get back as soon as I can."

"Be careful."

"Yes." He knew she was controlling herself with difficulty. He could tell by the tremor in her voice. He also knew that as soon as he left, she would burst into tears. He took her face in both his hands and kissed her lightly on the mouth. "It is going to be all right. I promise you."

A sob caught in her throat. He wanted to stay with her while she wept, but he knew he didn't have the time. He turned and disappeared into the darkness, hearing her muffled weeping behind him even before he was out of hearing.

He hated mobs because when men join together to form one they submerge their own consciences and become an entity that is without conscience. But what was happening now in Broken Butte was worse, even, than a mob. These men were acting in cold blood, willing to murder four innocent people to keep from facing the consequences of what they had done five months ago. Passion and anger he could understand and even, sometimes, forgive. But not this awful cold-bloodedness.

He made his way quickly through town, staying in alleys and darkened passageways whenever possible. Once, a dog came rushing out, barking furiously, as if he would attack. Cragg lunged at the dog, swung his revolver and heard the quick yelp as it struck the animal's head. After that he ran, swiftly, tirelessly and nearly silently because he knew the dog's barking might have drawn the men who were hunting him.

He began to think of Clara Easterday. Even if she survived the next few hours, remaining in Broken Butte would be impossible. If she and Cragg and the sheriff survived, ten men were going to have to pay the penalty for what they had done. The town would never forgive Clara for her part in that. She'd have to leave, and it might be a long time before she would even be able to sell her house and restaurant.

He felt responsible. But it wasn't a sense of responsibility that made him determined to help her when she left. He wanted Clara Easterday. He wanted to marry her. He hadn't known her long but something had happened to him that had never happened before. He was forty-five and he'd known his share of women but never before had one made him feel that life without her would be empty and meaningless.

He shook off thoughts of Clara impatiently, knowing they would dull his alertness and might get him caught. He avoided two men, one of whom was carrying a lantern, without difficulty. They were searching the town for him. That meant Carberry might be alone.

He reached Carberry's house by way of the alley, moving even more silently and cautiously than before. Gun in hand, he approached the stable, seeing light coming through some of the cracks.

He peered through one of them but could see nothing. He rounded the stable, carefully easing his weight down each time he took a step. Finally he came to a wider crack, through which he was better able to see into the dimly lighted stable.

Carberry sat on an overturned nail keg. Nan sat in a pile of loose hay. Two other men lounged between Nan and the door. There might be more but if there were he couldn't see them. He didn't see the sheriff but that didn't mean he wasn't here.

He stood there hesitating for a time. He could risk bursting into the stable and trying to take Carberry and the other two by surprise. Doing that would almost certainly result in some gunplay, which would bring the men searching the town for him back at a run.

He would, provided he was successful, have rescued Nan and probably Horsley as well but the trouble was that none of them would be able to get away. The stable would be instantly surrounded and they'd be prisoners just as surely as Nan and Horsley were now.

He withdrew as silently as he had approached. There had to be another way. Maybe if he returned to where Clara was, and let Carberry's men finish searching the town for them, there'd be a chance of eventually getting Carberry alone. They would undoubtedly search Clara's stable, along with her house. They'd discover that both team and buckboard were gone. They might assume that the pair had left town and make preparations for trailing them when daylight came. Maybe then, when most of the men were out of town trailing the buckboard, he'd get a chance at Carberry. And a chance to rescue Nan.

Cautiously but as swiftly as possible, he retraced his steps toward the place he had left Clara Easterday, troubled for no reason he could explain by an overpowering uneasiness. He began to hurry, worried that the searchers had somehow found her and taken her prisoner despite the fact that the buckboard was tethered some distance from the town.

The buckboard loomed up ahead of him and he called softly, "Clara?"

He received no answer. He halted, peering around him into the darkness. He studied the outline of the buckboard, dim in the starlight, looking for the hidden shapes of men. He called again, "Clara? Mrs. Easterday?"

Still no answer. He angled away from the buckboard and made a complete circle of it. The uneasiness had grown stronger. They must have found her and taken her prisoner. But if so, where were they? Why hadn't they stayed to try taking him?

The buckboard was, as nearly as he could tell, deserted. Finally, gun ready and cocked in his hand, he approached it, reached it and found that it really was.

Then the truth dawned on him. She hadn't been captured. She had gone into town and deliberately surrendered herself so that she could be with Nan.

He cursed angrily beneath his breath. What Clara had done had been foolish and unnecessary and had placed Nan in even greater jeopardy than before. Yet he couldn't bring himself to blame her. Surrendering herself had been courageous even if it had not been smart.

Now he was the only thing standing between Clara, Nan, Horsley, and the death Carberry had planned for them. If he was caught there would be no hope for any of the four.

He stood there hesitating, trying to decide what he should do. The smart thing would be to go for help. He could unhitch the buckboard horses, take one of them and ride bareback along the road the stage had used coming here. There was a town about forty or fifty miles east where there was a telegraph. He could get a message out for help and then wait until it arrived, calling, if need be, upon the local law-enforcement officer for help in case the Broken Butte lynchers arrived looking for him.

That would be the sensible, practical thing to do. That was what he would ordinarily do. The trouble with that course was that he had become personally involved. He was in love with Clara Easterday. He couldn't desert her because he knew it was possible Carberry would get rid of her, and Nan, and Horsley and then try claiming that Cragg was out of his head from the heat. Maybe he wouldn't get away with it, but it would be too late for Clara and Nan. They'd be dead, their bodies hidden.

He began to pace back and forth in the darkness, scowling angrily. Another alternative occurred to him. He could leave here on one of the buggy horses, leaving a trail that any fool could follow, and try to pick them off one by one tomorrow when they followed it. The chances of success using that plan were good, but it had the same flaw the first plan had. It exposed Clara, her daughter, and the sheriff to deadly danger and even if it succeeded did not guarantee their survival.

Neither plan was acceptable. Which left only one alternative. Alone, he must go back into Broken Butte. Alone, he must take on Carberry and the nine men who had participated, with him, in the lynching five months ago. Somehow, he had to separate Carberry from his men, and kill or capture him. Maybe with Carberry gone, the others, leaderless, would give up and surrender their hostages.

He admitted that there wasn't much chance of success. Having admitted that, he left the buckboard where it was and headed back toward town, afoot.

Clara Easterday waited nearly half an hour after Cragg had left. For a while, she sat on the buckboard seat, shivering despite the sultry heat of the night. Then she got down and began to pace back and forth.

She was terrified for Nan, and did not delude herself that the men of Broken Butte wouldn't harm the girl.

It was true that they were self-respecting, law-abiding men. It was also true that they were facing long terms in Yuma Penitentiary and that their own guilt over what they had done was intolerable. They were no longer rational, peaceful members of the community. They had become animals, fighting for survival. They were capable of doing things that would have been unthinkable to them six months ago. They were capable of murdering Nan and the sheriff in cold blood.

She had promised Cragg she would wait for him here, but suddenly she knew she couldn't wait. Nan was in danger, while she was free, and this was a situation no conscientious parent could tolerate.

She hurried toward town, relieved now that her mind was made up and she could finally do something. They would probably be holding Nan at Carberry's, she thought.

She thought about August Cragg. She visualized his face. He wasn't exactly a young man, but then she wasn't a girl herself.

He had been strongly attracted to her. She had seen that much in his stare of frank admiration, and smiled faintly to herself as she remembered it. In Broken Butte, people pretty much took her for granted, including the single men, most of whom had tried, at first, but who had stopped trying when she showed no interest in them. The kind of admiration Cragg had shown her warmed a woman and made her feel like a woman again.

If they all survived this night, and if he wanted her, she would go with him. She would uproot Nan and give up the comfortable existence she had enjoyed in Broken Butte even though Cragg was an unknown. She had been attracted to him as strongly as he had been to her.

She remembered the way her heart had speeded up under his warm and very personal regard. She'd felt like a schoolgirl again and she was a mature woman who had a daughter nearly fifteen.

It was pleasant to feel like a schoolgirl again. It would be pleasant to have a man hold her in his arms again, and to hear his heavy tread within the house. It would be nice to welcome him when he came home, and to have someone mature to talk to and cook for and eat with. And by no means least of all, it would be nice to have a man to sleep with again. That thought made her face feel warm and she thought how shameless she was and then she thought she wasn't being shameless at all but only remembering the years of loneliness and wanting it to end. She was a young woman yet with a lot of her life left to live, and August Cragg was offering a chance to live it with him. Or at least she thought he was.

She had entered one of the streets of town without realizing it, so preoccupied had she been with her thoughts. Suddenly she heard scuffling, running feet but before she could react she was seized from both sides and a harsh voice asked, "What are you doing here? Where's that marshal at?"

The voice belonged to Seward Littlejohn.

She said stiffly, "Please let go of me. I don't know where Mr. Cragg is."

"We ain't going to let go of you. You just come along with us. And you better tell us where that marshal is. It'll go easier on you if you do."

"I said I don't know where he is and I don't. I can tell you where he went, though. He went to Stover to telegraph for help."

There were three men in this group. The one who held the other arm asked, "Now what do we do? He'll be back with half a dozen marshals before forty-eight hours have passed. And maybe with a troop of cavalry."

Littlejohn said, "Shut up. Let's take her to Carberry's. Let him decide."

Clara asked, "Is that where you're holding Nan?"

"How do you know we're holding Nan?"

"She's gone. Who else would be holding her?"

"All right. That's where she is. And that's where you'll be until that marshal decides to give himself up to us."

"How can he do that? He's gone to Stover. I told you that."

"That don't mean we believed you. Just come on. We'll see what Carberry thinks of what you got to say."

CHAPTER 19

August Cragg had been a lawman all his life. Many times he had gone up against superior odds, even if he'd never gone up against odds of ten to one.

In that lifetime of working behind a badge, he had learned one thing. Criminals respect force. They have overwhelming respect for overwhelming force.

He was not going to come out of this alive by using half measures. Nor were half measures going to save the lives of Clara and her daughter, or that of the sheriff. The only chance Cragg had of saving his own and their lives was to strike terror into the hearts of the members of the lynch mob and keep it there.

Which left only one course of action open to him. He must become a scourge, a silent, unseen killer, taking vengeance against one after another of the lynchers until he had killed enough of them to throw terror into the hearts of those that remained.

He entered the town at the intersection of First and Cottonwood, in the northeast corner of the town. Here, both streets petered out as they left town, ending in weeds through which there was only a narrow path.

Cragg needed an advantage and he suddenly knew what would give it to him. He approached the nearest stable, standing behind a house that faced south on the corner of Second and Willow.

A horse nickered softly as he pulled open the squeaking

door. He felt his way to the animal, untied the halter rope and led the horse outside. He took the halter off, released the horse, then swiftly went back inside. There was a pile of loose hay in one corner. He lighted a match and dropped it into the hay.

He waited only an instant in the growing fire's yellow glare, but long enough to satisfy himself that there was enough hay in the pile to insure the wall of the stable catching fire. Then he left quickly. He moved silently along Willow toward Main, and hid himself behind a clump of tall bushes with withered but still faintly fragrant clusters of blossoms. He was far enough from the fire so that he could successfully hide himself, close enough so that he could identify men running toward it.

The blaze in the stable grew, confined so far to the interior. No sound save for that of the crackling fire broke the silence. A red glare came from the stable's open door. Suddenly he heard a scream, and shortly after that heard a man bawl, "Fire! Fire! Somebody ring the bell!"

No sound answered the man's shout. He came running around the corner of the house and, in bare feet and flapping nightshirt, ran toward the center of town where the courthouse was. Cragg waited. He briefly regretted the necessity of destroying an innocent man's stable as he watched the woman standing in the yard staring helplessly at the growing flames.

Uptown, the bell in the courthouse began to clang. A murmur of sound began to grow all over town. Cragg tensed himself, knowing the first ones to arrive would be those already awake and dressed—the lynchers gathered up at Carberry's or searching the town for him.

Two men came around the corner, running hard. The woman saw them and began to scream at them to hurry. They came abreast of where Cragg had concealed himself.

He raised his gun. Holding it in both hands to steady it, he took aim at the legs of the man in the lead. He fired, saw the man go down as if his legs had been cut from under him. He wasted no time, already having a bead on the legs of the second man.

The second man dropped beside the one who was down, not understanding what was happening. Cragg's bullet, aimed at his legs, caught him squarely in the chest. He collapsed over the wounded man and lay still, while the man whose leg had been hit tried to push him away. The woman began to screech even louder now, pure terror in her screams.

Cragg left his hiding place and hurried up the alley between Second Street and Main. He didn't stop until he was two blocks from the burning stable. Then he entered a passageway between two stores and shortly came out on Main.

People were running down Main toward the lower end of town. Cragg glimpsed Kubec standing in the open door of the stage depot. He wished he had a rifle but he did not.

He did have a wall beside him where he could steady the barrel of his gun. He eased around until he was comfortable, then aimed his revolver carefully at Kubec, steadying it with his left hand beneath the barrel and pressed hard against the building wall.

He tightened his finger on the trigger. Someone ran between him and his target and he did not fire. He glanced up the street. No one was closer than fifty feet so he took aim again and this time squeezed off his shot.

The distance was too great for any certainty in aiming. He'd only been able to aim at Kubec's body without being able to aim specifically at any part of it.

Kubec howled and disappeared so quickly that it was impossible for Cragg to know where he had been hit. The approaching man halted as suddenly as if he himself had been shot. He was wearing pants and shoes but no shirt. His nightshirt had simply been tucked into his pants. He had been in bed and therefore could not be one of the lynchers.

Cragg turned and hurried back along the passageway as fast as he could go. He heard the man in the street shouting frantically, "Hey! Somebody just shot Kubec!"

The murmur of sound from the direction of the fire had grown and so had the fire. Flames now shot into the sky for twenty feet, visible above the rooftops of the buildings between Cragg and the blaze. Besides the roar of the flames there was the mingled sound of shouts and, from the courthouse, the monotonous clanging of the firebell. Dogs barked incessantly and somewhere Cragg could hear the crying of a child.

He ran into a pile of tin cans and fell. He got up instantly and, gun still in hand, ran on up the alley to Maple Street. It wasn't far from here that they had tried beating him to death with a singletree. He eased along Maple, knowing that now they wouldn't bother trying to capture him. They'd shoot him down on sight.

Nor would those trying to kill him be limited to those who had taken part in the lynching. As soon as Kubec and the other two men were found, everyone in town would be hunting him.

But an anger of his own was building in him now. This course of action, distasteful as it was, had been forced on him. They'd forced his back against a wall and had given him no other choice. It had come down to choosing between the lives of Clara Easterday, her daughter Nan and the sheriff, and those of the men who had lynched two innocent drifters five months ago, and who were now trying to save their own skins even if it meant more murders of innocent people.

It wasn't much of a choice and Cragg had experienced no trouble making it. But shooting from ambush went against his grain and was contrary to everything in which he believed. It angered him that they had been able to force it on him.

He turned up Main, went past Clara Easterday's house and headed for Carberry's. Behind him, the flames were dying down. He heard a yell, "There he is! Anybody but him would be running toward the fire instead of away from it!" Guns flared in the bushes on the south side of the street. Cragg veered sharply to one side and headed for the concealment of the bushes and trees on the other side.

Something that felt like a red-hot iron burned along his thigh. He had been shot before and he knew exactly what it was. His leg buckled under him and sent him down on his face and chest, skidding in the dust. Someone yelled, "You got him!" and he heard footsteps running toward him, scuffing in the gravel of the walk.

He snapped two quick shots at the sound, and was rewarded by a yell of pain. The man stopped running toward him and sought cover in bushes and behind a picket fence. Once more their guns flashed, and once more bullets struck near him and in back of him, some of them ricocheting away, whining, into space.

Cragg got to his feet as quietly as he could. Tentatively he put his weight on the wounded leg and found that it would support him. It had been only momentarily numbed by the bullet and had given way, but it was all right now except for the bleeding, which had already reached his boot.

He needed to get away and he needed to look at his wound. If he tried to keep going, he might bleed to death or he might be weakened sufficiently to become easy prey for them.

There was only one place that he could go. Clara Easterday's. He backed away silently between two houses. Spasmodic firing still came from across the street. He turned back toward the center of town, knowing they'd expect him to head for Carberry's house. In the alley, he broke into a shambling run and only when he reached Maple Street did he turn north again.

He reached Main and stopped, hidden by high bushes on the corner lot. They had stopped shooting farther up the street. He crossed Main as quietly and as quickly as he could, and kept going until he reached the alley behind Clara's house. He turned into it, made it to her back gate and went in. He reached the back door and entered, wary and determined, in case they had set a trap for him here, to sell his life as dearly as he could.

But no one was here. He locked the back door behind him by silently shooting the bolt and then stood there, trying to remember where the flour-sack dish towels had been.

Recalling that they had hung on a rack beside the stove, he felt his way to them. He pulled all of them off the rack, then groped until he found the table and the lamp sitting in the middle of it. He had to have light to see how badly he was hurt and to properly bandage the gunshot wound. But he didn't dare let any light show through the windows or he'd never get out of the house alive.

The pantry. He remembered where it was and went to it, dragging a chair along with him. He took the chair inside, closed the door and lighted the lamp. He put it on a shelf, sat down in the chair, slit his pants with his knife and looked at his leg.

The entry wound was small and bluish, but where the bullet had exited the flesh was ragged and torn and it was from here that all the blood had come. Still, he was lucky. The bullet hadn't hit the bone and it hadn't severed any artery. The leg would hurt and it might even give way if he tried to run on it, but if he was careful he ought to get along all right.

He folded one of the towels, made a pad and placed it over the exit wound. He bound the pad in place with strips torn from the other towels, getting it tight enough so that it wouldn't come undone, not tight enough to cut the circulation off.

When that was done, he tied other strips around his slit pants leg to hold it in place and to keep it from flapping when he ran.

There was a brown bottle of whiskey on the pantry shelf. He uncorked it and took a drink. He took another, blew out the lamp and came out of the pantry into the kitchen.

He had killed one of the lynchers and had wounded at least two. He had cut the odds to seven to one, which was still too high. He had set a fire, and by doing so might have turned people against him who'd had nothing to do with the lynching five months ago.

He was going to lose unless he could get Carberry. As long as Carberry was egging them on, playing on their fears, they'd keep hunting him and trying to kill or capture him. As long as Carberry was alive, Clara's, Nan's, and Horsley's lives would be in jeopardy.

By feel, he replaced the spent cartridges in his gun. He opened the back door and stepped outside. Turning uptown, he headed for Carberry's house again.

CHAPTER 20

Cragg couldn't remember ever having felt so bad in his entire life. It was now early in the morning. He'd had no sleep. He'd been battered with a singletree and his head still ached abominably from that. His shoulder ached from the blows it had taken from the same instrument. His wounded leg was a fierce area of pain that stabbed him like a knife whenever he put his weight on it.

All he really wanted was to lie down and sleep around the clock. But he wasn't going to get a chance to sleep. Not until this was over with.

The blaze he had started had died and now put out only a feeble glow. Apparently the firefighters hadn't even tried to extinguish it. They had satisfied themselves with keeping it from spreading to anything else.

The townspeople would be returning to their homes, leaving only a few behind to make sure no wind scattered sparks and started fires elsewhere. For that reason he knew it would be reasonably safe for him to move around openly. He would be taken, in the darkness, for just another towns-man going home.

Carberry was the one he wanted and maybe now would be as good a time as any for going after him. At least three and maybe four of the lynchers had been shot. Others were probably out roaming the town looking for him. Carberry might be practically alone.

He headed for Carberry's house, staying as far away from

the other townsmen as possible so that he would not be recognized. At Maple, he left Main Street and entered the alley between Main and Third.

Limping silently up the alley, he saw cracks of light coming from Carberry's stable. He saw the shape of a guard silhouetted against those cracks of light. He froze thirty or forty feet away, listening. He could hear Carberry's voice and could make out enough of Carberry's words to get the gist of what was being said.

Carberry was instructing three of his men to take Clara, Nan and the sheriff to Clara's house. They were to be hit on the head and the house fired by spreading coal oil liberally over everything. He told the men to let the fire get started well before ringing the firebell. Carberry, finishing his instructions from the door, said plainly, "When he sees that fire, Cragg will show himself. Just be ready, that's all. He set that one fire and he shot three men. It won't be hard to convince folks that he just went berserk."

The three men herded Nan, Clara, and the sheriff through the yard toward the front of the house. One of the men was limping, one of those he had shot, thought Cragg. He tried to figure the odds up in his mind. One of the ten lynchers was dead. Three were with the hostages. If he assumed the wounded ones were still functioning, that left Carberry and five of his men. One was standing guard outside the stable. As many as four could be inside with Carberry.

Cragg told himself, "One thing at a time," and approached the guard as stealthily as he could, conscious that he didn't have much time. He had heard Carberry give the order for Clara's, Nan's, and the sheriff's deaths. It would be carried out promptly. It might even be hastened if the sheriff put up a fight.

Aware of this urgency, he rushed the last couple of yards,

risking the chance that his leg would give out on him. He struck the guard just as the man saw him, just as he called out with alarm.

He was brutal and efficient. His gun was coming down even as his body struck the man and the cry of alarm was cut off before it was scarcely out of the man's mouth. Cragg let the unconscious man fall and came around the corner at a shambling, limping run. No time now for finesse or care or even ordinary concern for his life. He burst into the door of the stable, taking in the scene instantaneously.

Carberry stood in the middle of the room. A man with a slit pants leg and a bandage on his leg sat on the edge of the grain bin. Another man was in the act of getting up from an overturned nail keg. A fourth, the most dangerous, had a gun in his hand, leveled at the door.

Cragg fired instantly from a distance of only half a dozen feet. He couldn't miss. The bullet took the man squarely in the chest and flung him back as if he had been kicked by a mule. He fell against Carberry, throwing him aside and knocking him to the floor.

The man rising from the nail keg now had his gun up. He saw Cragg's smoking gun muzzle swing toward him even as, from the corner of his eye, he saw the dead man fall. He opened his mouth to cry out, to give himself up, and he let his grip on his gun relax so that it could fall to the floor.

His attempt to surrender came too late. Cragg's bullet was already on its way. It took the man in the throat, cut off his cry and knocked him backward, sprawling, over the nail keg and onto the manure-littered floor.

The man on the edge of the grain bin yelled frantically, "I give up. Don't shoot!" and flung his gun away as if it was very hot.

Cragg stepped across to him, watching Carberry on the

floor trying to get his hands and knees under him. He clipped the man who had surrendered on the head and coldly watched him fall, saying, "I can't afford to take a chance on you."

Carberry looked up at Cragg from his hands and knees. Cragg said, "Get up. You and I are going to Mrs. Easterday's and you're going to stop your men from setting it afire."

Carberry, his face gray with fear, got cautiously to his feet. Cragg jabbed him in the back with his gun muzzle cruelly, savagely. Carberry grunted but he moved out the door at a shambling gait somewhere between a walk and a run. Cragg came along behind, never letting Carberry get more than a couple of feet ahead.

Through the yard they went, turning right at the street and crossing diagonally toward Clara Easterday's house. Cragg realized he had been holding his breath, waiting to see if the fire already had been set. But the house was dark.

Which didn't mean he was in time. At any instant fire might race through the house, following the coal oil, turning the place into an instantaneous inferno in which nothing could survive.

Reaching the front of the house, he yanked Carberry to a halt and jammed his gun muzzle into Carberry's ear with enough force to make the man grunt with pain. He said, "Call out! Tell them!"

Carberry hesitated only an instant. Then he bawled, "Go ahead! Burn it!"

Cragg's finger was tight on the trigger. He didn't know why he didn't just pull it and have it over with. But he didn't. Instead he slashed savagely with the gun, catching Carberry just above the ear. Carberry collapsed without a sound. Running frantically toward the house, Cragg knew why he hadn't killed Carberry just now. He'd wanted the man to go to trial. He'd wanted him sent to Yuma, or hanged if anything happened to the three hostages inside Clara's house.

He ran up the walk, just as the first flare of flame lighted the square that marked the open door. He burst inside.

The three who had brought Clara, her daughter, and the sheriff here were crowding toward the doorway. When they saw him framed in it, they stopped and grabbed for their guns.

Cragg shot the first one in the stomach. He fell sideways and tripped the second one, who yelled, "No! Don't shoot!"

Cragg nearly killed him, so unmanageable was his fury now. Only the knowledge that he needed help stopped him from doing so. He yelled, "Get back there and drag one of them out!"

The man hesitated for the barest instant. Then, flinging away his gun, he turned and ran toward the room where the fire was.

The remaining man, who had been slow getting his gun out, now dropped it and followed the other one. Cragg waited even though he was terrified for Clara's safety until both men reappeared. One was dragging Nan, whose dress was smoldering. The other was dragging the sheriff.

Cragg holstered his own gun and scooped up the guns the three had dropped. He ran into the blazing room where Clara was, flinging the guns away as he ran toward her. Her dress was also smoldering and she was surrounded with blazing coal oil.

He seized her under the arms, burning his hands, ignoring it. There was a bruise on her forehead from which blood oozed. He dragged her clear of the flames and stopped long enough in the parlor to crouch and beat the fire out with his hands. Then he dragged her out the door into the cool early morning air.

The grass was damp with dew and he rolled her in it until the last spark in her dress was out. Carberry still lay where he had fallen. The other two men had disappeared.

But others were coming now and the firebell in the courthouse was clanging for the second time tonight. Weary, half-dressed people came hurrying to fight the flames but could only stand and watch.

Hebert, the town doctor, knelt beside the unconscious but still living hostages on the dew-damp grass.

The sheriff stirred as the doctor held something to his nose. He struggled to a sitting position and the doctor went to Nan. She revived and he came to where Clara was.

He glanced at Cragg, at his blackened face and singed hair. He examined the bump on Clara's head. "She's going to have a headache. But she'll be all right."

Cragg nodded. Beyond the doctor he could see that the eastern sky was turning gray.

The doctor said, "It's been like a sore, festering. Now maybe it can heal."

Cragg knew what he meant. The doctor went away to look at Carberry. Clara opened her eyes and looked up at August Cragg.

He'd never expected to see that look in the eyes of any woman. They were filled with a glorious joy just to see that he was still alive. He glanced up for an instant to see the rim of the sun poking itself above the plain. He looked back at Clara. There were a lot of words to be spoken, but now was not the time. Their eyes were saying to each other everything that needed to be said.